EDITH & MR. BEAR

DARE WRIGHT

Houghton Mifflin Company
Boston

To my generous and loving voluntary Godmother

The text of this book is set in 17-point Bodoni Book.

Originally published by Random House, Inc.

This title was originally cataloged by the Library of Congress as follows:
Wright, Dare. Edith & Mr. Bear.
1 v. (unpaged) illus. 33 cm.
I. Title. PZ7.W935Ed   64-20565
RNF ISBN: 0-618-00332-0 PAP ISBN: 0-618-04253-9

Manufactured in the United States of America
LBM 10 9 8 7 6 5 4 3 2 1

At the foot of the stairs, where they could watch the front door, sat Edith and Little Bear.

They were waiting for Mr. Bear to come home from a trip.

"I wish that he'd hurry up and get here," said Little Bear.

"Be quiet, Little Bear. I'm reading to you," said Edith.

"I wonder if Mr. Bear will bring us a present," said Little Bear.

"Of course he will," Edith said. "He always does."

Just then the front door opened, and on the threshold stood Mr. Bear with his luggage and a large package. Little Bear nudged Edith. "Look, it's a big present!" he said.

But the package wasn't for them.

There *were* presents for them — a sailboat for Little Bear
and a party dress for Edith.
"Oh, Mr. Bear, it's a long dress! Oh, thank you. Look,
Little Bear, I have a long dress," cried Edith.
"My sailboat's better than a silly dress," said Little Bear.

Edith couldn't wait to put on her dress.

"Do hurry with the buttons, Mr. Bear," she begged.

"I want to see how I look."

Little Bear couldn't wait to try out his sailboat.

"Now it's my turn," said Mr. Bear, cutting the string of
the mysterious big package.

"Please, Mr. Bear, what's in it?" asked Edith.

"Just wait and see," said Mr. Bear.

"Come on back, Little Bear. Mr. Bear is going to open
his parcel now," called Edith.

"Look out, Little Bear,"
said Edith. "Your old boat
is dripping all over my
new dress."
But she forgot all about her
dress when Mr. Bear got the
package open.
Inside was a clock.
Edith had never seen such
a clock.
The sides were made of
glass. You could see the
pendulum swing, and watch
the wheels go round.

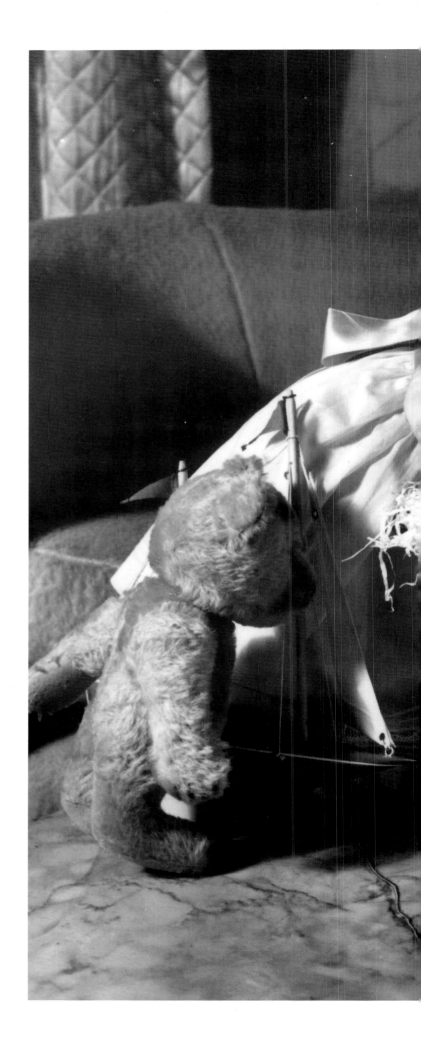

"This is a present for me," said Mr. Bear.

"Who gave it to you?" asked Little Bear.

"I gave it to myself," said Mr. Bear.

"Where are you going to put it?" asked Edith.

"On the mantel," said Mr. Bear.

"But that's so high up," said Edith. "We won't be able to see the wheels go round."

"It'll be safe there," said Mr. Bear.

And that's where the clock went — right in the middle
of the high mantelpiece.
Edith was always stopping to stare up at it. She loved
to hear the hours chime, and to watch the slow swing of
the pendulum.
"I wish I could touch it, Kitten," said Edith.

So one day when she
was alone Edith built
a stairway of chairs and
books, and climbed
up to where she could
touch the clock.

She turned it around, opened the back, and put
her hand in.
When she touched the pendulum, it stopped.
Edith snatched her hand out so fast that she lost
her balance.

She teetered on the pile of books, grabbed at the clock
to save herself, and down with a crash came Edith and
the clock together.
Edith wasn't hurt.

But nothing was left of the clock except broken glass
and wheels that didn't go round.
All Edith could think of was how to hide the dreadful
thing that she had done.
As fast as she could, she put away the books.

She took a mop, and swept the bits of clock under the
logs in the fireplace.
Then she ran and hid in her room.
"Maybe Mr. Bear won't notice right away," she thought.

But Mr. Bear noticed!

"Edith! Little Bear! Come here at once," he roared.

"Which of you broke this clock?"

"I didn't," said Little Bear.

Edith opened her mouth to say "I did it," but the words didn't come. She shook her head.

"Very well," said Mr. Bear, gathering up the broken pieces, "but whichever one of you is lying isn't going to be very happy. You're sure you didn't do it, Edith?"

Edith looked away. She swallowed. "I didn't do it,"
she said.

Mr. Bear was right. From then on Edith wasn't a bit happy.

She didn't feel like playing with Little Bear.

She couldn't keep her mind on her lessons.

"Two and two don't make five, stupid," said Little Bear.

"I know," said Edith. "I was thinking about something

else." What she was thinking about was the clock.

She didn't even enjoy her birthday party, although she
wore her new dress and had a cake with candles.
"Oh, Kitten," she said, "you're the only one I can tell.
I broke the clock, and if he knew it Mr. Bear would
never have given me a birthday party at all. He'd hate
me. Everybody would hate me."

She quarreled with Little
Bear.
"What do you think of my
painting, Little Bear?" she
asked.
"It needs more orange," said
Little Bear.
"It does not!" said Edith.
She stepped back to look,
and kicked over a paint pot.

"You've ruined my drawing,"
howled Little Bear.
"You did it yourself, and you
can't draw anyway," said
Edith, and she slapped him.
"I don't like you. You're
horrid," shouted Little Bear.
"I never want to play with
you again!"

"It was all my fault," thought Edith, when Little Bear had rushed away, clutching his spoiled drawing. "I *am* horrid. I get horrider every day. Pretty soon nobody will like me. Maybe I should run away."

The more Edith thought about it the better the idea seemed.

"I'll go right now," she decided.

She changed into her outdoor clothes.

She stole quietly out of the house.

She ran and ran, and soon the streets around her were
all unfamiliar.

She fell and skinned her knee.

Lunchtime came, and there was nothing for her to eat.

She was tired and cold. She cried herself to sleep beside
an ash can, and woke wondering where she was.

When Edith was missing at lunch Mr. Bear began calling all the neighbors. No one had seen Edith.

"She was mean to me this morning, and I got mad at her. I haven't seen her since. I'm sorry, Mr. Bear," said Little Bear.

"There, there," said Mr. Bear, although he was really very worried. "I'm sure she's all right."

"Who are you going to call now?" asked Little Bear.
"The police. They'll soon find her. She must be near
by," said Mr. Bear.

But Edith wasn't near by. She had gone on until she came to a great river lined with piers. At one pier a ship was getting ready to sail.

It was a very big ship indeed. "It's so big that it must be going far away," thought Edith. "If I could sneak on board it would take me far away, too, and I would never, never have to tell Mr. Bear that I was the one who broke his clock."

Then she thought that never, never would she see
Mr. Bear and Little Bear again!
She burst into tears.
"I want to go home," she cried.

But how could she go home?

"I could if I told Mr. Bear the truth about the clock,"
thought Edith.

So she dried her tears and set out for home.

Dusk was beginning to fall before Edith found her own
street again.

The house door stood ajar, and she crept in.

Mr. Bear was pacing anxiously up and down the living
room, with Little Bear at his heels, when a bedraggled
little figure appeared in the doorway.

"I've come home," said Edith, "and, Mr. Bear, there's
something I have to tell you."

"Now, now, no talking until we get you warm and clean
you up. You're a mess, Edith. Wherever have you been?
We've been frantic," said Mr. Bear.

He popped her right into the bathtub.

"Lots of soap, Edith, and scrub hard," said Mr. Bear.

"But I have to talk to you," said Edith.

"All in good time," said Mr. Bear, drying her.

"But, Mr. Bear, I have to tell you now."

"Hot milk next," said Mr. Bear.

"I can't drink it. Not until
I tell you," said Edith. "Oh,
Mr. Bear, I did it. I broke
your clock. And now you
won't love me any more."

"Well, now, I always thought
it was you. I've been waiting
for you to tell me. Why
did you lie about it, Edith?"
asked Mr. Bear.

"I loved the clock so much.
I never meant to hurt it. I
only wanted to touch it, and
I broke it all to pieces. I just
couldn't tell you," said Edith.

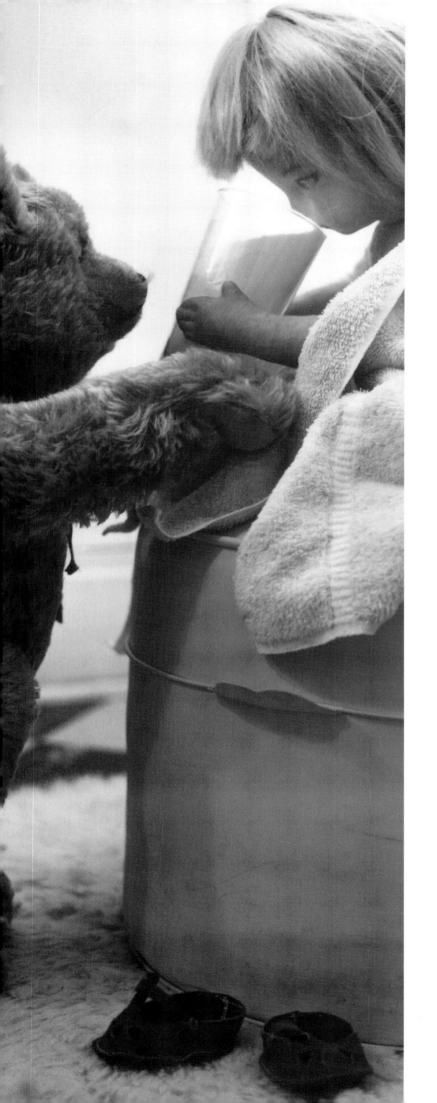

"It was naughty of you
to touch the clock without
asking me, Edith, but I
know you didn't break it
on purpose. I wouldn't
have punished you for an
accident. If only you had
told me the truth," said
Mr. Bear.

"I wish I had," said Edith.

"And you were very unfair to Little Bear. What if I had blamed him for it?" asked Mr. Bear.

"I know," said Edith. "How are you going to punish me?"

"I'm not. I think you've already punished yourself," said Mr. Bear.

"I'd feel better if you punished me," said Edith.

"I know you would," said Mr. Bear, "but I believe you've learned your lesson. I don't think you'll lie again. Now into bed with you."

"Oh, Mr. Bear, I do feel so much better," said Edith as Mr. Bear tucked her in. "You don't hate me — really and truly?"

"Don't be foolish, Edith. Of course I don't hate you," answered Mr. Bear. "Go to sleep."

Edith went to sleep happy.

And she woke up happy.

"Oh, Mr. Bear, everything is so nice today. I love
everybody," Edith cried.

"All right, but be careful of my glasses," said Mr. Bear.

"I love you most of all, dear Mr. Bear," said Edith.

"Thank you," said Mr. Bear, "but don't choke me, Edith."

"Don't ever tell a lie, Little Bear," said Edith.

"I didn't," said Little Bear.

"I'll never do anything bad again," said Edith.

"H-m-m," said Mr. Bear.

"I'll be good forever and ever," insisted Edith.

Of course she wasn't!

She and Little Bear got into all kinds of mischief.
There was the time that Edith suggested digging up the
daffodil bulbs which Mr. Bear had just planted. She
wanted to see if they had begun to grow yet.
They hadn't, and Edith and Little Bear quickly planted
them all again — upside down!
"I can't understand why those daffodils never came up,"
said Mr. Bear in the spring.

There was the time Edith decided to cook a surprise
for Mr. Bear.

"You're making an awful mess," said Little Bear.

"All good cooks make messes," Edith said. "Hand me
the salt, Little Bear, and then we'll light the stove."

"All right, but you know what Mr. Bear has told us
about using matches," said Little Bear.

"I can't cook without a fire," said Edith.

"I just hope Mr. Bear doesn't catch us," said Little Bear. Mr. Bear did catch them! He turned them both over his knee right then and there. "You might have burned down the whole house with us in it," growled Mr. Bear. "Don't ever dare touch matches again!"

There were all the times that Edith boasted about her
adventures the day she had run away.

"Little Bear, did I ever tell you about sleeping beside
the ash can all by myself?" asked Edith as they were
walking through the park one day.

"Only about a hundred times," said Little Bear. "Let's
sail my boat."
"That's only a toy boat. You've never seen a real boat
like the huge one that I was on the time I was going to
sail far away all by myself," said Edith.

"Edith," said Mr. Bear, "what was that you said about being on a boat?"

"Well, the boat I thought about getting on," corrected Edith quickly, because never again did she tell Mr. Bear a lie.

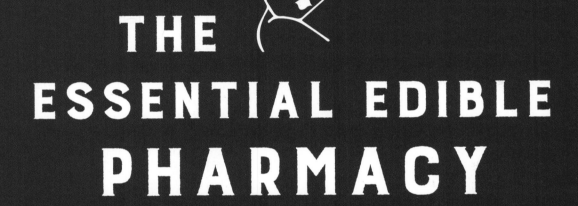

THE ESSENTIAL EDIBLE PHARMACY

heal yourself from the inside out

SOPHIE MANOLAS

EXISLE PUBLISHING

Community Learning & Libraries
Cymuned Ddysgu a Llyfrgelloedd

This item should be returned or renewed by the
last date stamped below.

H+W

£6
07/06/17

E

BLE

Y

To renew visit:
www.newport.gov.uk/libraries

ABOUT THE AUTHOR

Sophie Manolas is a clinical nutritionist, whose country childhood taught her the importance of the home vegetable patch and fresh produce from an early age. She was inspired to study Nutritional Medicine after a long struggle with Polycystic Ovarian Syndrome — a change in diet proved to be the only effective treatment. After qualifying as a clinical nutritionist, Sophie established her own practice, specializing in women's health and hormonal issues, and has achieved great success with her down-to-earth approach and comprehensive understanding of how we can use food as our medicine. Her own property is established on permaculture principles, with Sophie and her partner growing and producing the majority of their food themselves.

Sophie is extremely down to earth, with 'tried and true' approaches (quite literally) to maintaining a healthy and yummy lifestyle. Thank you for all your wisdom — offering organic, healthy and **realistic** *options for me to adopt in my everyday life!*
Eliza C.

I had an interest in and respect for the role of nutrition in health, but I was lost and confused with all the information out there and felt I was getting unhealthily fixated on certain ideas. I am so thankful I came across Soph! She has such deep knowledge that is balanced with the recognition of the influence of other lifestyle factors on nutrition for health. The insights she offers consistently help me step back and see the bigger picture, and present so many 'ah but of course' moments. The information and strategies she offers are always presented in a very accessible, balanced and realistic manner. And you can't help but be enthused by her happy, energetic passion! I have limitless appreciation for her, for the care and time she has given me. I treasure any titbit of knowledge I get from Soph (her Facebook and Instagram in particular are amazing!) and this book will be no exception.
Josh R.

Consumed by an abundance of free health advice offered on the Internet, I often find myself confused by every opinion I see. Luckily, after my first consultation with Sophie Manolas, I immediately warmed to her friendly, non-pretentious take on health and nutrition. I now seek out Sophie's advice on a regular basis and would highly recommend others do the same.
Romain D.

I tell you what ... [Sophie is] the food goddess! Informative in a sense that people like me can understand food and its benefit in simple terms. [She's] a legend!
Cherie R.

[Sophie] changed my life, [she is] one in a million. Thank you for all of your time and effort; I look forward to my healthy active life ahead.
Nathan N.

Sophie Manolas is a wonderful talent who has helped me on multiple levels. Her writing is engaging, extremely funny and personal. The woman behind **The Essential Edible Pharmacy** *has a heart of gold, she is down to earth and truly cares for people around her. I am so pleased that she has published her first book, it is a huge acquisition for society. Sophie is a nutritionist who provides her readers with thought-through recipes and gives us an insight to why certain foods can change our health in both positive and negative ways.*
Emma H.

CONTENTS

Introduction

Good nutrition is the cornerstone of good health. Regularly eating various, abundantly nutritious foods is the single most important thing you can do to prevent risk factors for major diseases, as well as looking and feeling your absolute best throughout life. And it tastes incredible too! Eating lots of 'living' foods full of important macro and micronutrients makes you *feel* alive and is one of the most valuable things you can do for yourself, and teach your family and children about. Eating well is the starting block for anything we do in our lives. As Grandma always says, 'health is wealth', and there is plainly nothing more important than that. But this needn't mean routine drudgery or a boring diet; eating really, really well can be a tasty adventure. This book is designed to educate and inspire you to get into the kitchen and eat your way to being the greatest, healthiest and most sustainable version of yourself.

THE SCIENCE

For millennia, people have been using medicinal foods to influence their health. More recently, evidence-based research has been able to break down the exact nutrient elements of foods in order study precisely what the mechanism is that contributes to the prevention and management of human diseases and ailments. What we now know about the influence diet can have on health is mind-blowing, and the best part is that nutritional sciences are advancing all the time.

What you put in your mouth can have an enormous influence on the digestive tract and the balance of healthy gut flora, which has been scientifically proven to affect all kinds of conditions from mental health to immune response (80 per cent of our immunity comes from the gut) and how you break down and digest your food, making its nutrients available for the body to use. Numerous studies into the prevention of cancer have pointed to naturally occurring nutrients in foods, and it is widely scientifically acknowledged that vitamin C can have a huge effect on the immune system, as can the allicin compound in garlic. Vitamin A is proven to be essential for great skin. The beauty of these nutrients occurring abundantly in our commonly available foods is that often, nutrients are packaged together and work synergistically to have positive effects on the body.

Whether you have an ailment you'd like to manage with the help of nutrition, or you're just looking to live your best life full of energy and vital health, nutrition is always the starting point.

A BIT ABOUT ME

I am a clinically trained nutritionist fanatically passionate about food: the growing and production of food, the failures and triumphs and alchemy of cooking food, and most importantly, of course, the consumption of food!

After completing my qualifications, I now manage my own nutrition clinic. As well as my clinical clients, I also develop corporate wellness programs and run workshops for different community groups, from new mums to the elderly.

My own experiences with health through nutrition have been life-long, growing up mainly as a vegetarian and seeing how one kind of diet affects people differently nutritionally, and then struggling with the symptoms of Polycystic Ovarian Syndrome and managing my condition easily with some basic dietary changes despite conventional medical treatment detrimentally affecting my health (with no reduction in symptoms).

Nutritional science is constantly evolving. Every day new breakthroughs are being made and developed in human health and it is not only my job but my passion to keep up to date with the latest developments, as well as researching and debunking new diet trends and weighing up their pros and cons for the individual. What we now know about human health and its relationship with diet is phenomenal, and there is nothing I would rather spend my time doing than reading up on developments and analyzing the latest studies.

WHY
The Essential Edible Pharmacy?

The Essential Edible Pharmacy takes a broad and comprehensive look at commonly available foods and examines how they can contribute to maintaining great health and preventing the onset of disease. This is aimed at simplifying the process of making the best dietary choices, and to show you that all whole foods, in their own way, are 'superfoods'. The book identifies the available nutrients in these common foods and what conditions they can be helpful for. Treat this book as a guide on the most nutrient-dense common foods and exactly *why* they are so good.

The foods selected herein represent the most widely available foods at local supermarkets or growers' markets all over the western world. The aim is to fully understand the nutritional value of easily recognized foods and to guide you towards eating the humbler vegetables again because their nutritional power is phenomenal! We all know leafy greens are great for us (and I explain exactly how), but it is mind-blowing how nutrient-dense plain old green beans are. How incredibly nourishing root vegetables are. And I explain the best way to prepare the foods in order to get the greatest nutrient value from them, as well as how foods can be combined to increase their nutrient content.

My own experiences with these foods are documented in the book: my absolute love affair with cooking and the different treatments of food, learning about how the cooking process can enhance or deplete the nutrient content of the food, and growing my own vegetables in my permaculture garden at home including interdependent vegetable crops and animals (such as chickens and Muscovy ducks), which is self-sustainable and for the most part is where my partner and I source our food. This is, in my opinion as a nutritionist, an extremely important factor in gaining the highest nutritional value from food, and I would love for food production to be a seed within the minds of everyone who reads this book. But it doesn't have to be that complex; my philosophy is always to grow what you can, especially herbs, which are a cinch to grow (for the record, I've grown carrots and celery in pots on an apartment balcony), but it is perfectly okay to source your fresh fruits and vegetables from the growers' market or supermarket too.

HOW TO USE THIS BOOK

The Essential Edible Pharmacy is an easy-to-understand look at the differing nutrient profiles of common foods, walking through separate fruits, vegetables, nuts, legumes, herbs and spices, grouped into classifications for ease of reference. Each ingredient is highlighted individually with what makes it special, and a simple recipe is included for each ingredient. You can use this information in any way you wish: hopefully it inspires you to incorporate at least a few of these wonderful ingredients in your everyday cooking, if not all of them!

As you make your way through the recipes, here are a few points to keep in mind.

- Always adjust the amounts for seasonings to your own particular taste.
- Where possible it's best to use organic ingredients, including fruits, vegetables, honey, eggs and meat.
- When buying maple syrup, make sure it is 100 per cent maple syrup (not 'maple-flavoured' syrup).
- Eggs, meat and fish should ideally be pastured, free range or sustainably sourced. This is not only for the wellbeing of the animal, but it also has an effect on the nutrient content of the food. For example, pastured eggs typically have greater levels of omega-3 fatty acids than their pellet-fed caged counterparts.
- Use fresh herbs and fresh lemon juice when you can.

Oven temperatures

°Celsius (C)	°Fahrenheit (F)
120	250
150	300
180	355
200	400
220	450

Volume equivalents

Metric	Imperial (approximate)
20 ml	½ fl oz
60 ml	2 fl oz
80 ml	3 fl oz
125 ml	4½ fl oz
160 ml	5½ fl oz
180 ml	6 fl oz
250 ml	9 fl oz
375 ml	13 fl oz
500 ml	18 fl oz
750 ml	1½ pints
1 litre	1¾ pints

The following standard baking tins have been used for the recipes in this book:
Cake – 20 cm (8 in.) diameter
Tart – 25 cm (10 in.) diameter
Loaf – 28 x 13 cm (11 x 5 in.)

Weight equivalents

Metric	Imperial (approximate)
10 g	½ oz
50 g	2 oz
80 g	3 oz
100 g	3½ oz
150 g	5 oz
175 g	6 oz
250 g	9 oz
375 g	13 oz
500 g	1 lb
750 g	1⅔ lb
1 kg	2 lb

Cup and spoon conversions

1 teaspoon = 5 ml

1 tablespoon = 20 ml

¼ cup = 60 ml

⅓ cup = 80 ml

½ cup = 125 ml

⅔ cup = 160 ml

¾ cup = 180 ml

1 cup = 250 ml

1. Leafy GREENS

Leafy greens will save your life.

There is almost no ailment that a daily dose of leafy greens won't help remedy in the long term. It was a long-standing joke back in my university days that the first dietary prescription for almost every client was 'increase leafy greens'... it is one of the most powerful dietary bases for a preventative diet.

When choosing your leafy greens, no matter the variety, look for bright, fresh, vital colouring, and leaves that are slightly 'crunchy'. Limp leaves will have started to oxidize and won't contain the same high levels of antioxidants and nutrients.

I have found leafy greens the easiest perennials to grow at home, some even in pots.

The bitter varieties — rocket (arugula), chicory (witlof/Belgian endive), dandelion, radish and mustard greens — are invaluable to your health, aiding digestion by increasing hydrochloric acid levels in the stomach, reducing heartburn and aiding the second phase of liver detoxification. They are also an essential addition to a self-sustaining organic permaculture garden, as they deter pests and vermin from eating your crops. Talk about multi-talented.

ROCKET (ARUGULA)

Let's start things right with my old friend rocket. Rocket is a gorgeous perennial leafy green of the brassica family that I eat almost every day, both because it is hugely abundant and overgrown in my garden, and because it is a superstar ingredient packed head-to-toe with essential nutrients.

Rocket is a peppery, slightly bitter leafy green, and if the taste is a little strong for your preference, try eating the younger leaves. The more mature the rocket grows and the larger and darker green the leaf, the more bitter and peppery the taste.

A powerhouse of nutrition, rocket contains beta-carotene (the precursor to vitamin A), vitamin C, vitamin K, iron, and B vitamins including folate (vitamin B9), which is critical for healthy conception and the early stages of pregnancy and is essential for the activation of its other friends amongst the B-group vitamins.

Rocket is also very high in antioxidants responsible for cancer prevention, particularly in the prevention of cancers of the reproductive organs like cervical, ovarian, breast and prostate cancers.

the benefits

healthy reproductive system, pre-conception & pregnancy

❋

immune function

❋

cancer protective

❋

skin health

NIN'S ZESTY ZOODLES

2 large zucchini
(courgettes)

juice of 1 lemon, but have
another ready, just in case

sea salt and pepper, to taste

2 red chillies
(chili peppers), thinly
sliced (deseeded if you
prefer it not too hot)

3 cloves garlic,
peeled and finely grated

¼ cup extra virgin olive
oil, plus a little extra for
sautéing

100 g (3½ oz) parmesan
cheese *or* 50 g
(3 tablespoons) nutritional
yeast

100 g (3½ oz) rocket
(arugula) leaves — tender
baby leaves are best for this
recipe

Nin (Nate) is my eldest brother. He and his wife are easily the best cooks who ever walked this Earth. I'm talking about the kind of kitchen wizards who butter toast and it is the greatest thing you ever put near your face. Nin has never cooked anything that ever tasted bad, even when we were kids — he couldn't if he tried. His skills are definitely not genetic, because I can cook exactly half as well as he can.

This is my attempt at healthifying his incredibly simple chilli (chili pepper), rocket (arugula) and lemon pasta. His version uses traditional wheat pasta (which he makes himself) and a bucket of parmesan cheese as big as his head. My version uses a little more restraint and a serious increase in vegetable content. Both taste amazing. Rocket adds an irreplaceable peppery freshness to the dish.

SERVES 2 AS A MAIN;
ALSO MAKES A QUICK AND TASTY SIDE DISH

First, make 'spaghetti' out of the zucchini. This can be done with a commercially available spiralizer; alternatively, slice the zucchini into long, thin strips to resemble 'noodles' or pasta with a kitchen machine or mandolin, or with a vegetable peeler and a light hand.

Next, in a small bowl, whisk together the lemon juice, salt, pepper, chilli, garlic and half the olive oil. Taste often and adjust if desired. When the four main ingredients of oil, lemon, chilli and garlic are in the right balance, this basic dressing will really sing. It shouldn't be too mild or oily, not too tangy garlic, not too zingy lemon ... to use a Goldilocks cliché, each must be just right. If it doesn't taste great with your finger dipped in the bowl, it won't taste amazing as a completed dish. Now, warm your zucchini noodles in a hot pan with a little oil to stop them burning (1 tablespoon will be more than enough). Once warm but not cooked to the point of falling apart (they should have the texture of al dente pasta), take the pan off the heat, add the dressing and stir through. While still off the heat, stir through the parmesan cheese, then add rocket leaves and stir through again. Ensure all ingredients are very well combined.

Serve while still warm.

the benefits

healthy bones and joints

✳

energy production

✳

heart health

✳

immunity

SPINACH

A regular nibble of spinach helps so many conditions in some way, due to its sheer abundance of nutrients and the body systems they are indicated in assisting (i.e. all of them).

Spinach delivers a massive dose of vitamin K (for bone and digestive health), vitamin A (for a healthy pregnancy, skin and immunity), manganese (for healthy joint maintenance and repair), B complex vitamins (for energy production and as a co-factor for countless functions in the body, particularly B9 for a healthy pregnancy), magnesium (for muscles, physical and emotional health, to aid a good night's sleep, and for bone health), calcium (for bone health), vitamin C (for glowing skin, wound repair, immunity), fibre (for weight regulation) and potassium (for heart health), and a bunch of lutein, a carotenoid lauded for maintaining eye health. In fact, spinach contains various other anti-cancer carotenoids, too, as well as being loaded with antioxidants and the power to reduce inflammation all over the place. Spinach is one of the most outrageously nutritious foods out there.

It is important to remember to eat both raw and cooked spinach. Spinach contains oxalic acid, a naturally occurring organic compound found in lots of different foods. Oxalic acid is destroyed by heat, but when eaten raw it can block the absorption of nutrients. The other side of that coin is that the cooking process, while destroying oxalic acid, also destroys some of the fabulous nutrients in spinach like vitamin C, and leaches away some of its mineral content. So to get a good balance, mix it up! Raw baby spinach is a great base for a salad, for example, or you can sauté it in some coconut oil a la Garlicky Greens on page 195.

THE LOWDOWN: INFLAMMATION

Inflammation is a normal part of the body's immune response. It helps to immobilize the damaged area and begin the healing process. Inflammation becomes a problem when this response gets out of control, or systemic throughout the body, especially in auto immune conditions like arthritis. This heightened immune response stresses the body's immune system as it constantly fights to alleviate unwarranted inflammation and requires nutrients that your body could be using elsewhere.

SPINACH, SWEET POTATO AND QUINOA BURGERS

2 cups cooked quinoa, cooked (refer to pack), drained and cooled

4 handfuls chopped fresh spinach (100 g/3½ oz if using frozen)

1 cup pre-cooked and cooled sweet potato (steamed/boiled is fine)

4 eggs

¾ cup rolled (porridge) oats

chopped herbs and spices, to taste, e.g. paprika, chilli (chili pepper), parsley, oregano and basil

coconut oil, to shallow fry

MAKES 8–10 PATTIES

Place all ingredients into a bowl, then mix and massage with the hands until completely combined. Allow the mixture to set in the fridge for 20 minutes.

Remove the mixture from the fridge. Form patties by taking a couple of tablespoons of mixture into your hand, rolling into a ball and pressing flat. Place a frying pan on the stove, add a couple of tablespoons of coconut oil and fry in the hot pan.

Serve hot as a bunless burger wrapped in an iceberg lettuce leaf, with slices of tomato, cucumber, red onion, pickle and avocado.

MUSTARD GREENS

the benefits

glowing skin

✳

strong bones

✳

cancer protective

✳

anti-inflammatory

Lovely little lacey mustard greens have a similar nutrient profile to their cruciferous brethren: they contain a massive dose of vitamin K (which is anti-inflammatory and especially effective for digestive inflammation), vitamin A precursors (for healthy pregnancy, respiratory health, antioxidant, gorgeous healthy skin, immunity and a healthy pregnancy), vitamin C (for wound repair, antioxidant, skin health, immune function, cancer prevention, amongst many other functions), manganese (a powerful antioxidant and great at keeping joints healthy, like oil on the Tin Man), absorbable calcium (for bone health), vitamin E (antioxidant, skin health, immunity), fibre (detoxification and weight management, bowel health), plus iron (and the vitamin C to absorb it) and B complex vitamins.

This wondrous cacophony is like a nutrient punch in the face (in the best possible way), and eating a little of your mustard greens each week will really set up your body for stages one and two of detoxification (see 'The lowdown' on p. 29), cancer prevention, fighting harmful inflammation and fighting the ageing process. Mustard greens are particularly valued for their extreme dedication to kicking cholesterol's ass: they contain phytonutrients called glucosinolates, which aid the excretion of cholesterol from the body. (Thanks, mustard greens!) They also contain a wealth of other incredible phytonutrients, the most incredible of them all being quercetin, a comprehensive compound that aids the treatment of so many ailments they are too numerous to name here.

Mustard greens are especially easy to grow at home and will deter pests, being a 'bitter' leaf (they actually taste more peppery, like rocket/arugula, than bitter). A side salad of mustard greens with some really good olive oil is wonderful enough for me as they have such a unique and delicious flavour of their own. But if you want to mix it up, behold my Peppery Pesto recipe — a spoonful on some fresh, homegrown cherry tomatoes is, honestly, extraordinary.

THE LOWDOWN: IRON ABSORPTION

Non-haem (non-heme) iron is the iron that we predominantly get from plant sources, while haem (heme) iron is the type we obtain from animal sources, particularly red meat. Plant-based non-haem iron is not as readily absorbed by the body as the haem iron from animals, but non-haem iron absorption is hugely increased when consumed at the same time as vitamin C. Vitamin C binds with the non-haem iron in order to be absorbed in the duodenum.

In order to get the most out of your plant-based iron sources, include some vitamin C-rich foods like a squeeze of fresh lemon juice over some sautéed spinach or some raw red capsicum (pepper) in a mustard green salad.

PEPPERY PESTO

¼ cup pepitas
(pumpkin seeds)

¼ cup sunflower seeds

½ cup macadamia nuts

sea salt and pepper, to taste

3 cloves garlic,
peeled and chopped

3 cups mustard greens,
tightly packed

1½ cups extra virgin
olive oil

MAKES APPROXIMATELY 2 CUPS
NOTE: THIS RECIPE REQUIRES SOAKING TIME

In a bowl or jar, cover pepitas, sunflower seeds and macadamia nuts with filtered water. Leave for at least 3 hours — I leave mine overnight. Soaking is not strictly essential, but makes for a much lovelier, creamier consistency. If you have a very high-powered processor at home (powerful enough to make smooth nut butters) then this step may not be necessary if you're pressed for time.

Rinse and drain, then pop into the bowl of a food processor with the sea salt, pepper and garlic. Blend until combined. Then add the mustard greens and blend again. Slowly add the extra virgin olive oil while processing until your pesto is the perfect consistency. Your pesto should be creamy and able to be scooped out without falling off the spoon.

Brassica FAMILY

Brassica vegetables are the wonderful group of plants that are here to beautify us with their selenium and vitamin C, assist liver detoxification with their sulphuric compounds and boost our immune systems while helping to protect against cancer with their powerful antioxidants. The brassicas are amongst the most nutritious of all the healthy wholefoods, so try to incorporate these into your diet at least four times a week for an all-round health boost to heal what ails you.

the benefits

*good for almost
everything!*

✳

healthy digestion

✳

energy production

✳

strong, healthy bones

✳

anti-inflammatory

✳

cancer protective

KALE

Kale has earned a pretty hilarious reputation recently as a
hipster superfood. But let me tell you a thing: the hype is
real and it is deserved! Kale has a nutrient profile as long as
your arm. It contains many of the nutrients found in other
leafy greens, plus a few extra, including vitamins K, A, C and
B-group, loads of fibre, calcium, potassium, iron, vitamin E,
magnesium, protein and omega-3 fatty acids and a bunch
of flavonoids and carotenoids. What a beautiful thing is the
kale plant — literally. Have you seen a purple curly kale?
It's so beautiful I want to make a suit out of it and wear it
around. Alas, I can only wear it in my belly, and be all the
better off for it.

A regular chow down on kale will help the body to fully
and properly detoxify, keep cholesterol levels in balance, and reduce the risk of cancer. It
is cardio-protective, antioxidant and strongly anti-inflammatory, also protecting against
inflammation of the stomach lining by protecting against the overgrowth of *Helicobacter
pylori* bacteria, the most common cause of stomach ulcers.

There are a few varieties of commonly grown and available kale, all of which are a
breeze to grow at home in your own garden, and can be a real ornamental feature. Our kale
has grown over head height and, once well established, we even stopped watering it! So it

is rather low maintenance, especially when planted amongst some pest-repellent rocket (arugula) or mustard greens and marigolds.

The tough, woody stalks contain a lot of insoluble fibre, but not a lot of nutrient, so if you are just starting to include kale in your diet or don't particularly enjoy the stalk, simply chop it out and consume the softer part of the leaf. Or slice the leaves extra-thin, as in the recipe here for Kale Chopped Salad.

. . . .

KALE CHOPPED SALAD

1 bunch kale (curly, Tuscan, whatever is available)

1 x 400 g (14 oz) can cannellini beans, thoroughly rinsed and drained

1 x 400 g (14 oz) can lentils, thoroughly rinsed and drained

1 red onion, chopped

¼ cup linseeds/flaxseeds

¼ cup sunflower seeds

100 g (3½ oz) cherry tomatoes, halved

100 g (3½ oz) goat's cheese or feta cheese

1 avocado, chopped

equal parts sesame oil and lemon juice *or* unfiltered apple cider vinegar, to dress

SERVES 2 AS A MAIN MEAL
OR 4 AS A SIDE SALAD

Wash and pat dry the kale. With a sharp knife, remove the stems from the centre of each kale leaf then slice the kale into very thin ribbons; the thinner the better. This will make the kale into lovely, soft noodle-like strips that will soak up the dressing (to help absorb all that fat-soluble vitamin A and K!)

Next, in a large bowl toss the cannellini beans, lentils, onion, linseeds/flaxseeds, sunflower seeds and cherry tomatoes. Top with the cheese and avocado, then dress and serve.

Serve especially to those who refuse to eat kale. When chopped super-fine as in this recipe, the fibrousness of the leaves that makes them less palatable to some is negated. This salad takes no time at all to throw together, and is a lunchtime staple in our household (mainly due to rampant kale growth in the veggie patch, but also because of the simple yet wonderful flavours and nutrient balance).

the benefits

overall health

✳

weight control

✳

beautiful skin

✳

heart health

✳

digestive function

BROCCOLI

Broccoli (or 'trees' as my five-year-old self would refer to them) are one of the healthiest foods you can put in your body. Their lovely green foliage holds a wealth of beautiful nutrients including vitamin K, vitamin C, lots of B-group vitamins including a heap of folate, vitamin A, vitamin E, manganese, choline, chromium, potassium, omega-3 fatty acids, magnesium, iron, calcium, protein, zinc and selenium. Broccoli contains other vitally important phytonutrients like antioxidant kaempferol, which is highly anti-inflammatory and fantastic at reducing allergic reactions, and important glucosinolates, which are vital for detoxification processes in the body. Broccoli also provides lots of fibre to further assist the detoxification process and digestive function.

Being so rich in so many incredible macro- and micronutrients, there are few things that a regular dose of broccoli won't help to prevent or alleviate, but if you are simply maintaining good health, this beautiful vegetable is going to help maintain gorgeous skin, keep your cholesterol in check, your bones strong and healthy and your heart in good working order. Broccoli florets and stems are beautiful roasted then topped with tahini dressing, steamed with a little sesame oil or blanched and cooled then tossed into a salad. The raw florets can also be chopped up finely to add beautiful crunch and colour (and nutrients) to a regular salad.

SIMPLE SPECIAL STIR-FRY

2–3 tablespoons
coconut oil

400 g (14 oz) organic
pastured beef, cut into
strips (you can substitute
400 g/14 oz wild raw
prawns/shrimp)

1 onion, sliced

4 cups broccoli,
cut into florets

1 cup raw cashew nuts

1 teaspoon–1 tablespoon
chilli flakes, according to
heat tolerance

1 red capsicum (pepper),
cut into strips, seeds
discarded

1 carrot, julienned

1 bulb garlic, peeled and
chopped (correct — an
entire bulb)

2 tablespoons tamari sauce

sesame seeds, to serve

sesame oil, to serve
(a little goes a long way)

juice from 1 lime,
to serve

coriander (cilantro) leaves,
to serve

Just 5 minutes of preparation is required for a glorious mid-week, throw-together dinner.

SERVES 4

Place a wok over a *hot, hot* heat and add the coconut oil. Add the beef and sizzle for 2 minutes (if using prawns/shrimp, add them at the same time as the vegetables so they don't overcook). Now add the onion, broccoli, cashew nuts, chilli flakes, capsicum (pepper), carrots and garlic all at once. Carefully move the ingredients around in the pan, so they flash cook without burning.

Once all the ingredients are cooked through (about 5 to 6 minutes), add the tamari sauce and stir through, then remove from the heat. Divide among four bowls or plates and sprinkle on some the sesame seeds, sesame oil, lime juice and coriander leaves. This is a lovely light meal with a wonderful injection of nutrients.

CAULIFLOWER

The humble cauliflower has to be one of the hardest working vegetables out there. For somebody transitioning to a lower refined carbohydrate or paleo way of life, it is a dream ingredient — it can be used to make pizza bases or as a substitute for rice, and makes a more delicious mash than potatoes.

Cauliflower lends a big helping hand to many of the major functions in the body, including phases 1 and 2 of liver detoxification (see 'The lowdown' on the opposite page), brain function, heart health, digestion (it's a good source of fibre and has been shown to inhibit the overgrowth of *Helicobacter pylori*, the bacteria often responsible for gastric ulcers and gastritis). It contains a wealth of vitamins, minerals and antioxidant phytochemicals including vitamin C, vitamin K, B-group vitamins, magnesium, choline, omega-3 fatty acids, manganese, fibre and phosphorous.

the benefits

liver cleansing

❈

aids digestive health

❈

antibacterial

THE LOWDOWN: LIVER DETOXIFICATION

There are two main phases of detoxification that the liver goes through every day in order to process and safely get rid of compounds the body doesn't need or has utilized already, including hormones (both those made by the body and synthetic hormones), drugs and alcohol, some medications, industrial chemicals that might be present on our food (e.g. pesticides and food additives). In very basic terms, phase 1 of liver detoxification is where the liver cells facilitate a number of chemical reactions which turn the undesirable, potentially harmful contaminants and waste products into less harmful chemicals, ready for excretion. During phase 2 the substances are subjected to further chemical reactions, which render the undesirable substances water soluble and able to be excreted relatively easily via urine or bile.

Different nutrients can greatly inhibit or help both phases of liver detoxification, so make sure you eat a wide variety of vegetables to give your liver a helping hand!

CAULIFLOWER MASH

1 whole small head of cauliflower, or ½ a large one

2–3 cloves garlic, peeled and chopped

2–3 tablespoons butter *or* extra virgin olive oil

sea salt and pepper, to taste

optional: pinch of chilli flakes or cayenne pepper

SERVES 4 AS A SIDE

Cut off the bottom stem of the cauliflower then cut the head into florets or small pieces. Mix the garlic through the cauliflower, then steam or boil until soft and cooked through. Drain well, then tip into a large bowl. Mash with a potato masher just as you would for mashed potatoes. Add butter (or oil), salt, pepper and chilli flakes or cayenne pepper to taste, and serve.

CAULIFLOWER FRIED RICE

1 whole small head
of cauliflower,
or ½ a large one

1 onion, peeled and
chopped

2–3 cloves garlic,
peeled and chopped

1 carrot, finely chopped

½ capsicum (pepper),
finely chopped, seeds
removed

1 cup peas, shelled,
or chopped whole snow
peas (mangetout)

small bunch of spring
onions (scallion), both
white and green parts,
finely chopped

coconut oil, to sauté

1–2 tablespoons tamari
sauce

½ a lemon

optional: chilli flakes, to
taste

SERVES 4 AS A SIDE

In a food processor, blitz the raw cauliflower until it is broken down into pieces of a similar size to rice. Place a large wok or frying pan over a high heat then add the coconut oil. Add the cauliflower and the remaining ingredients, except the lemon juice, tamari sauce and chilli flakes, and sauté for 5 minutes until just cooked. Season with tamari sauce, 1 tablespoon at a time, until seasoned to taste (don't add too much at a time as it can get very salty), then squeeze a little fresh lemon over the top and add chilli flakes if desired.

Deeelicious and so very easy!

the benefits

anti-inflammatory

✽

liver cleansing

✽

cardio-protective

✽

healthy bones

✽

boost immunity

BRUSSELS SPROUTS

Brussels sprouts are the wonderful yet deeply misunderstood little green warriors of the vegetable world. If they are overcooked, they can taste slightly bitter, and this can sadly turn some people against them for life. The poor little darlings; all they ever wanted to do was give you many nutrients, help protect you from cancer and reduce your cholesterol.

Happily, brussels sprouts are enjoying a mini-resurgence as more people discover different ways to cook them beyond steaming or boiling them to a mushy pulp. When cooked nicely they add a gorgeous pop of flavour and texture to lots of dishes.

When given the chance, brussels sprouts bestow upon their consumers a huge range of essential nutrients including vitamin K, B-group vitamins, fibre, manganese, choline, potassium, omega-3 fatty acids, iron, magnesium, calcium, zinc and vitamin A precursors, as well as a wealth of sulphuric compounds to help the body's detoxification process. They are antioxidant, anti-inflammatory and cardio-protective, and they contain high levels of glucosinolates, the compounds responsible for brussels sprouts' cancer preventative reputation.

Sliced thinly and lightly pan-fried, brussels sprouts are a revelation in Lemon Mustard Green Salad with Poached Egg (see p. 101). Honey Roasted Brussels Sprouts are beyond lovely as a side dish or tossed into a salad.

HONEY ROASTED BRUSSELS SPROUTS

¼ cup coconut oil or extra virgin olive oil, to cook

500 g (2 lb) brussels sprouts, bottom woody part removed, cut into halves

1 or 2 onions, brown or red, cut into quarters

6 cloves garlic, peeled and chopped

2 tablespoons balsamic vinegar

2 tablespoons honey

sea salt and pepper, to taste

SERVES 4 AS A SUBSTANTIAL SIDE

Preheat the oven to 180°C (350°F). Place a large frying pan over a medium heat, heat the oil and pop in the brussels sprouts. Allow to cook until slightly browned, stirring occasionally. Add the onion and garlic and cook for a few more minutes until everything softens without burning.

Next, transfer everything to a roasting pan and shake the pan from side to side until the brussels sprouts are evenly spread out. Sprinkle with balsamic vinegar, then use a tablespoon to drizzle the honey over the sprouts so it is evenly distributed rather than concentrated in blobs, which may burn.

Roast in the oven for 15 to 20 minutes, and serve hot as a side or on top of a simple salad (even just on rocket/arugula leaves).

CABBAGE

Ah cabbages! Tightly packed, crunchy, tasty heads of anti-inflammatory, liver-loving power nutrients! Cabbages are a beautiful staple food in lots of cuisines, including beautiful belly-filling, heart-warming Polish, German, Greek, Russian, Japanese, Korean and Chinese dishes. Cabbage is delicious raw, cooked and fermented.

These wonderful vegetables are a parcel of nutrients, containing lots of vitamin K, vitamin C (when raw), manganese (for those squeaky knees! Manganese is great for joint health), potassium, fibre, B-group vitamins, copper, choline, selenium, magnesium, iron, calcium and protein. They also provide lots of highly antioxidant polyphenols (see 'The lowdown' below). These polyphenols, combined with the extra cancer-kicking glucosinolates in cabbage make for a fantastic health boost for all kinds of ailments in the body, from inflammatory digestive complaints like stomach ulcers to cardiovascular disease. Cabbage also packs the all-important glutamine, the amino acid which increases muscle mass (fantastic for weight management and degenerative diseases), prevents systemic infection and can help digestive issues from Crohn's disease to irritable bowel syndrome and diarrhoea.

Cabbages vary radically in flavour, from sweet to slightly bitter, and the different varieties offer up varying nutrient profiles, so be sure to include different varieties of cabbage in your diet, from gorgeous purple cabbage to savoy and plain run-of-the-mill green cabbage.

THE LOWDOWN: ANTIOXIDANT POLYPHENOLS

Antioxidant polyphenols are brilliant, naturally occurring micronutrients that have lots of incredibly important roles within the body, from influencing cell receptors and enzymatic activity, to preventing cancer formation and metastases, reducing the likelihood of degenerative diseases, lowering cholesterol and preventing cardiovascular disease.

KIMCHI

1 whole head of cabbage (any kind — I use red and green), outer leaves discarded, cut into squares approximately 2 cm x 2 cm (¾ x ¾ in.)

approximately ¼ cup sea salt (flakes or finely ground)

1 cup water

1 knob ginger, grated

5 cloves garlic, peeled and finely grated

4–5 tablespoons chilli flakes (or cayenne pepper, or a mix of both) *or* 1 red chilli (chili pepper), seeded, very thinly sliced

1 tablespoon honey

2 tablespoons fish sauce *or* 1 tablespoon water and 1 tablespoon tamari sauce

½ red onion, thinly sliced

2 radishes, thinly sliced

1 carrot, julienned

Kimchi is a great way to include cabbage in your diet. It's a wonderful probiotic fermented cabbage condiment originating in Korean cuisine, kind of a like a sauerkraut of the East. It is pungent, ever so slightly sweet, salty and spicy all at once, and a couple of tablespoons of kimchi spooned onto a simple salad, on top of a clear soup or with fish elevates the flavour exponentially, while also aiding the digestion of the meal as a whole. I make a great big batch of it and keep it refrigerated once it is nicely ripe (see the opposite page for fermentation times).

In a large non-reactive bowl, mix together the cabbage and salt — I do this by layering salt and cabbage — then massage quite firmly with your hands (nightmarish if you are sporting any papercuts; if this is the case, use gloves!)

Keep massaging for at least 10 minutes, or until the cabbage starts to give up its moisture (this will be apparent: there will be a watery substance in the bottom of the bowl). Squeeze and massage for a just a little longer, then add up to 1 cup of water, little by little. Now, place a plate or similar on top of the cabbage (one that will fit inside the opening of the bowl) and weigh down the plate with something heavy, such a large dictionary or a few cans from the pantry.

Let it stand like this, unrefrigerated, for at least 2 hours.

Transfer the cabbage to a colander and rinse well under cold water. Leave in the sink for 10 minutes, then shake to remove as much moisture as possible and repeat. This is to remove any excess salt. Leave the cabbage in the colander to drain.

Meanwhile, make the kimchi paste by mixing together the ginger, garlic, chilli, honey and fish sauce or tamari sauce and water. In a large bowl, mix together the salted cabbage, kimchi paste and other vegetables until really well combined. I mix with my hands — as before, if you have sensitive skin and/or papercuts you will want to wear gloves, and be *very* careful about whatever you touch as the chilli will cause pain if you rub your eyes, nose or go to the bathroom.

Place all the ingredients, including any liquid, into a large sterilized preserving jar. Pack the contents down carefully but very firmly so that the chilli brine rises above the vegetables. Ideally you will have about 1 cm (⅓ in.) of liquid above the vegetable mixture. Be sure to leave a little gap of at least 2 cm (¾ in.) of air at the top of the jar, as the mixture will bubble and expand as it ferments.

Leave your jar in a cool, dark place at room temperature. Check it every day and press the mixture down with a spoon if it rises to the top. The fermentation process will take anywhere from 48 hours to 5 or 6 days. Taste a little each day and if you like the taste, it is ready. It will become more strongly flavoured and pungent the longer it is left, so if you are new to the fermenting game, refrigerate your first batch after a shorter fermenting time. Your kimchi is ready to refrigerate and eat.

3.

Root
VEGETABLES

Containing complex carbohydrates, root vegetables are some of my favourite vegetables to suggest to people suffering from any kind of stress, including adrenal fatigue and exhaustion, anxiety and to aid in recovery for those who do a lot of weight training or aerobic exercise. They fill the belly, are incredibly versatile and are wonderful for helping to maintain a healthy digestive system by providing a food source for beneficial bacteria.

CARROT

My first thoughts when I think about carrots are always skin, eyes, respiratory health, pregnancy and breastfeeding health. Carrots are full of the beautiful antioxidant beta-carotene (see 'The lowdown' on the opposite page). They are one of the most fundamental, widely consumed vegetables. These brilliant orange (and purple, yellow and white) crunch sticks are incredibly versatile, sitting happily as a steamed side dish, roasted, as a dipping implement or adding fabulous colour grated into salads and savoury dishes to increase the vegetable content (you can grate carrot into bolognese sauce to bulk it out) and perhaps, most importantly, adding the moisture and sweetness to luscious carrot cakes.

Carrots are famously good at promoting great eyesight, thanks to their lutein content. They also provide a stack of other benefits, making them well worth regular inclusion in your diet. They help reduce the risk of cardiovascular disease and, thanks to their incredibly high content of vitamin A precursors, have been shown to be helpful in the prevention of lung cancer in particular. Many studies have looked at vitamin A in the prevention and reduction of lung tumours. While artificially produced vitamin A supplementation can make the disease worse, naturally occurring vitamin A and vitamin A precursors (like those abundant in carrots) have been shown to be incredibly important in the fight against and reduction of lung cancer. Carrots also contain vitamin K, fibre, potassium, vitamin C, B-group vitamins, vitamin E, copper and phosphorous, as well as powerful phytonutrients like falcarindiol and falcarinol. These compounds have been shown to reduce cancer risk, particularly colon cancer (thanks also to the fibre content). They are naturally occurring pesticides — the root vegetable's own-grown protection against pests and diseases, which luckily for us also seems to help guard against cancer too.

Carrots are at their very best eaten raw and with an element of fat to increase the absorption of their rich vitamin A content.

THE LOWDOWN: BETA-CAROTENE

Beta-carotene is a precursor to vitamin A. When healthy, our bodies convert beta-carotene into vitamin A, which is what I'm talking about when I mention 'Vitamin A precursors'. They're not fully fledged vitamin A, but they can be converted by the body into vitamin A. Beta-carotene gives pigment to orange, yellow, red and dark green fruits and vegetables.

CARROT CAKE

12 teaspoons chia seeds

2 cups (approximately
3 big handfuls) almond
or coconut flour (or a
combination of the two)

1 big handful of shredded
coconut

4 teaspoons ground
cinnamon

4 teaspoons
ground ginger

1 teaspoon nutmeg

⅔ cup maple syrup

⅔ cup coconut oil, melted

2 carrots, washed

1 big handful of walnuts

butter for greasing cake tin

ICING (FROSTING)

1 cup coconut cream
chilled overnight
(it needs to be solid)

optional: big handful of
shredded coconut
(I like it but it does make
your icing look lumpy)

optional: maple syrup and/
or vanilla seeds, to taste

In a small bowl mix the chia seeds with ½ a cup of water and allow to sit for at least 10 minutes while you grate the carrot. Preheat oven to 170°C (340°F). In a large bowl, mix together the flours, shredded coconut and spices. In another bowl, mix together the maple syrup, coconut oil and chia seed mixture. Then carefully add the wet ingredients to the dry, rhythmically stirring with a big wooden spoon (yes the rhythm is important). Once everything is mixed, taste it with your finger; taste it again. Taste it a third time (because there is nothing more wonderful in this life than raw cake batter) then add the grated carrots and walnuts. (Don't make the rookie error of adding the walnuts to the dry ingredients; the flour gets stuck inside the grooves of the walnuts, making it difficult to mix properly.)

Grease a cake tin with butter and line with baking (parchment) paper. Give the batter another mix, then spoon into the cake tin. Cook for approximately 30 minutes until the cake is golden brown and springy when poked in the middle.

Remove the cake from the oven and carefully turn it out of the tin. Let it chill on a chopping board or wire cake rack while you make the icing (frosting).

Spoon the coconut cream into a large bowl and whip with an electric beater until fluffy, like whipped cream. Then very carefully add your optional extras and fold them in with a butter knife. Wait until your cake is completely cooled to frost it, as a warm cake will melt your icing — for this reason, also keep refrigerated between eating sessions!

the benefits

beautiful glowing skin!

❋

cancer protective

❋

eye health

RADISH

Aside from being absolutely gorgeous to look at and providing a fresh, peppery crunch to salads, radishes are one of the most nutrient-dense root vegetables out there. They are widely considered to be the most beautifying of all the vegetables, thanks to their silica content, vitamin C and sulphuric compounds, all of which mean wonderful things for your skin.

Radishes are little red lovelies packed full of the aforementioned vitamin C, which increases collagen production and cell turnover, and heals inflamed skin. They also contain B-group vitamins, iron, magnesium, calcium and vitally important phytonutrients sulforaphane (studied for its effectiveness in fighting neurodegenerative diseases, cancer and digestive disorders), zeaxanthin (an essential eye nutrient that helps stave off macular degeneration and other age-related eye diseases), beta-carotene (vitamin A precursor, also wonderful for eye health, as well as immune function, health during pregnancy and glowing skin) and lutein (the other essential eye nutrient; it is antioxidant too).

Radishes range from extremely mild in flavour to full-on eye-watering pepperiness, and the leafy green tops, similar to turnip leaves, are a wealth of nutrients comparable to other leafy greens and most certainly deserve a regular place in the diet. If eating the greens, choose the younger, fresher, bright green leaves.

FISH TACOS WITH RADISH SALAD

SERVES 4 AS A MAIN MEAL

RADISH SALAD

4 radishes, tops trimmed off, bulbs finely chopped

1 red onion, finely chopped

1 avocado, cubed

1 bunch coriander (cilantro), leaves and stalks chopped

1 large ripe tomato, chopped

1 small Lebanese (short) cucumber, chopped

corn kernels from 1 fresh corn cob

sea salt and pepper, to taste

juice of 1 lemon or 2 limes

optional: full-fat natural yoghurt

optional: Refried Beans (see p. 66)

TACO SEASONING

equal parts paprika, cumin powder, cayenne pepper, dried oregano, garlic powder, sea salt and pepper

TACOS

2–3 tablespoons coconut oil

800 g (1¾ lb) sustainably caught firm white-fleshed fish, chopped into 1 cm (⅓ in.) cubes

1 onion, peeled and chopped

3 cloves garlic, peeled and chopped

8 crisp iceberg lettuce leaves, washed and dried (these make easy, healthy taco shells)

In a large bowl, assemble the radish salad by tossing all salad ingredients together and sprinkling liberally with lemon or lime juice. To make the seasoning, mix together all the seasoning ingredients in a small bowl and set aside.

Place a large frying pan over medium to high heat and add the coconut oil. Add the onion and garlic and sauté for a few minutes, then add the cubed fish. Stir constantly, taking care not to overcook the fish. When the fish is almost entirely opaque and cooked through, add the taco seasoning, mixing in 1 tablespoon at a time, and stir through until the desired level of seasoning is reached (have a taste to make sure it isn't too hot or mild).

Place two lettuce leaves face-up on each plate. Assemble the tacos by adding radish salad and fish to the lettuce 'cups'. Serve with a dollop of full-fat natural yoghurt and Refried Beans if desired.

BEETROOT (BEETS)

I am crazy in love with beetroot and always have been. I was never a breakfast person as a kid, but my dear mum would always force us to drink a freshly pressed juice of beetroot, carrot, apple and ginger every day before school. Love your work, Mama!

Although it has the highest sugar content of any veg (don't panic, it's got tons of fibre so it's not going to give you diabetes on its own) I still eat, on average, one fresh, grated and raw beetroot in a salad per week because it is super pretty, super yum and super packed with nutrition.

Beetroot has been shown to lower blood pressure within an hour when consumed as pure juice. It contains betaine (a compound that protects cells), is an antioxidant and is very anti-inflammatory. Raw beetroot has been shown to be cancer protective, with many studies showing that it helps to guard against pancreatic, breast and prostate cancers.

Beetroot is high in vitamin C (when raw), fibre, potassium, manganese, B9 ... the list goes on. It is also a big-time blood and liver cleanser (for this very reason it is great to drink a glass of beet juice during and after a viral infection) as it kicks over the liver's excretory phase 2 of detoxification and kicks the viruses out of your system! Thanks beetroot!

HOME-CURED BEETROOT (BEETS) SALAD

1 large or 2 small whole beetroots (beets), leaves trimmed (include the green leafy tops in the salad if desired; they taste great and are nutrient dense little lovelies on their own)

1–1½ cups good white wine vinegar

¾ cup extra virgin olive oil

sea salt and pepper, to taste

SALAD

leafy greens: beetroot (beet) greens, rocket (arugula), baby spinach, etc.

1 red capsicum (pepper), deseeded and sliced

1 red onion, peeled and sliced into rings

optional: 1 avocado, 1 cup raw walnuts, goat's cheese or feta cheese

SERVES 4–6 AS A SIDE,
OR 3 AS A MAIN MEAL

Fill a saucepan with water then place on the stove and bring to the boil. Turn the heat down to medium, then add the beetroot, ensuring there is enough water to cover them, and gently boil. Try not to overcook, but ensure they are cooked through — generally, cooking on a low to medium heat for 20 to 30 minutes should suffice; poke with a fork to ensure they aren't raw inside.

Once cooked, place the beetroot in some cold water and allow to cool. Once cool, the outer 'skin' should easily peel away with the fingers. Peel completely, then thinly slice the beetroot, either carefully with a very sharp knife, or with a mandolin. You want the slices to be no more than 2 mm (⅟₁₂ in.) thick, but perfection is not important. You don't necessarily have to keep them as whole rounds either; little half-rounds are fine and look just as gorgeous.

In a large bowl, layer the beetroot slices with alternate, generous splashes of white wine vinegar and extra virgin olive oil, plus sea salt and pepper to taste. Allow the beets to cure for at least an hour in the fridge (overnight is fine too).

Arrange all the salad ingredients in a large bowl or on a serving plate, then place the beetroot slices on top. Dressing is not necessary as the beets will contribute their own dressing of vinegar and olive oil; however, a splash of sesame oil wouldn't go astray. Add a generous serving of Crunchy Poppy Seed Gremolata (p. 143) on top if desired.

Another idea for cured beetroots: layer on top of a Spinach, Sweet Potato and Quinoa Burger (p. 14) and wrap in a lettuce leaf for a tasty bunless burger.

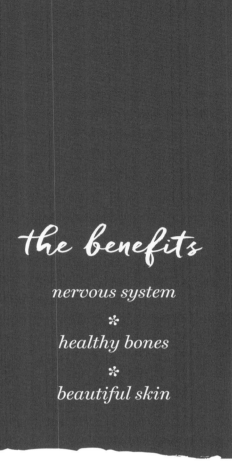

the benefits

nervous system

✱

healthy bones

✱

beautiful skin

PARSNIP

Parsnips are the new carrot; spread the word! These white, creamy, sometimes hairy-looking root vegetables are also a beautiful substitute for the more starch-laden common potato, and are much better for you.

Parsnips are seriously sweet in flavor and make beautiful chips or fries (see p. 52), and are also lovely pureed or roasted, and you can most definitely eat them raw, either grated into a salad like raw carrot or beetroot, or as a crudité. They contain a little omega-3 fatty acids, as well as vitamin C, vitamin E, B-group vitamins and choline (for brain and liver function, energy production, a healthy metabolism and nerve conduction). And they contain an impressive range of minerals including calcium and magnesium for strong bones, iron for red blood cells, potassium for heart health, zinc and selenium for gorgeous skin, immune function and reproductive health. They also contain beautiful antioxidant phytonutrients like falcarinol and falcarindiol, which have been shown to have anti-inflammatory, anti-fungal and anti-cancer properties, and lots of fibre to aid digestion.

Parsnips pair beautifully with lamb, chicken or fish, and are also perfect with garlic and made into a simple soup.

PARSNIP CHIPS (FRIES)

3 parsnips, tops cut off
and washed

coconut oil, melted

a seasoning of your choice:
I love smoked paprika,
dried thyme, chilli (chili
powder), cumin, fennel
seeds or sesame seeds,
or plain old sea salt and
pepper is great, too.

These chips are just brilliant because in one very simple recipe, you can combine all of the nutritional benefits we just spoke about, and with just three ingredients make a beautiful comfort food that is satisfying both for your tummy and your nervous system. These are easier than potato fries (which need to be double- or even triple-cooked) and come together in a matter of minutes.

SERVES 2 AS A SIDE

To prepare, preheat the oven to 180°C (350°F) and line a baking tray (baking sheet) with baking (parchment) paper. Chop your parsnips into quarters, lengthways, to make lovely, long wedges.

In a large bowl, mix together the parsnip wedges and coconut oil with your hands (ensure the oil is not too hot or you will burn your hands). Place the coated wedges on the baking tray, ensuring none are overlapping. (You want as much surface area of the chip to touch the baking tray; this will make the crunchiest chips!) Sprinkle with the seasoning of your choice, and pop into the oven.

Watch in amazement as they turn into golden wedges of greatness. After approximately 10 minutes, open the oven door and turn over the parsnip pieces with tongs. Parsnips caramelize quite quickly and can burn easily, so keep an eye on them. Check and remove from the oven after another 10 to 15 minutes.

Season and serve while hot!

the benefits

healthy bones

❋

energy production

❋

immunity

❋

skin health

TURNIP

For the first 25 years of my life, I really only ate turnips as part of minestrone soup. Which is a real shame, because this psychedelic tuber is good all over, from purplish root to bright green leaf.

The leafy tops of the humble turnip, though not commonly eaten, are as good as any other leafy green, providing a whole heap of vitamin K, antioxidant beta-carotene (vitamin A precursor), vitamin C, B-group vitamins, iron, manganese, fibre, absorbable calcium and vitamin E, as well as potassium and magnesium. You should most certainly start to think about including the leafy part of the turnip in your diet as you would any other leafy green, instead of relegating it to the chicken coop or worm farm!

The more common part of the turnip, the plump root part, is, I acknowledge, wonderful in minestrone soup. But it's also delicious as a puree with a little olive oil, garlic and pepper, or sautéed in some coconut oil with harissa paste (see p. 63) or curry spices, or simply as a roast vegetable like its other root vegetable buddies.

The root is rich in vitamin C (although this is destroyed the moment you cook it — but baby turnips can be sliced finely and eaten raw in a salad, trust me), fibre, calcium, potassium and magnesium.

VEGETARIAN SHEPHERD'S PIE

extra virgin olive oil

1 onion, chopped

6 cloves garlic, peeled and finely chopped

2 turnips, washed and grated

2 carrots, washed and grated

10 button mushrooms, cut into quarters

1 cup shelled peas

2 celery sticks, sliced into little 'c' shapes

2 teaspoons ground cumin powder

1–2 tablespoons garlic powder

4 ripe tomatoes, chopped *or* 1 x 400 g (14 oz) can chopped tomatoes

¼ cup balsamic vinegar

1 cup liquid vegetable stock

1 x 400 g (14 oz) can lentils, drained and rinsed

sea salt and pepper, to taste

2 medium-sized sweet potatoes, peeled, cooked and mashed, for topping

2 tablespoons sesame seeds

This recipe offers the perfect way to make use of the veggies in the crisper at the end of the week.

SERVES 4–6

Preheat the oven to 180°C (350°F). Place a large saucepan over medium to high heat and add a little olive oil, then add the onion, garlic, turnips, carrot, mushrooms, peas and celery and stir for a few minutes until cooked through. Add cumin and garlic powder and stir through. Then add the tomatoes, vinegar, stock and lentils. Stir and allow to simmer for 5 to 10 minutes, stirring occasionally, adding sea salt and pepper.

Spoon the mixture into a large casserole dish and level the top with the back of a spoon. Top with the mashed sweet potato. Level the sweet potato with a fork, creating some attractive looking grooves that will crisp up in the oven. Drizzle a little extra olive oil on top, then sprinkle on the sesame seeds that will add a little more crunch to the top of your shepherd's pie. Pop into the oven for 10 to 20 minutes until cooked through. Serve hot on a cold night for extra effect!

SWEET POTATO

Sweet potatoes are not the most attractive vegetable in the world. Even sweet potatoes themselves would acknowledge this. But sweet potatoes know that none of that superficial nonsense matters when you are packing such serious nutritious credentials.

These delicious tubers come in a range of colours, from the most commonly available bright orange to creamy white, yellow and deep, dark purple. The different colour varieties represent differing nutrient profiles. The bright orange sweet potatoes are one of the richest plant-based sources of provitamin A available, which is responsible for that rich, ochre colour, while the colour of purple sweet potatoes is caused by antioxidant anthocyanins. Both contain a wealth of other nutrients, too, like fibre, vitamin C, manganese, a range of B-group vitamins, phosphorous, potassium and copper. They're beautiful for maintaining energy levels thanks to their B vitamin and copper content, and contain slowly absorbed carbohydrates to restock glycogen stores after exercise, along with satisfying great hunger or a sweet tooth with their wonderful flavour and fibre/carbohydrate mix. Sweet potatoes are a great choice for diabetics, thanks to their blood sugar-modulating properties as a 'slow-burn' carbohydrate. All of that beautiful vitamin A is incredibly helpful for a huge range of health concerns from skin conditions to respiratory issues like asthma, to immune function and health during preconception and pregnancy.

Sweet potatoes aren't in the same family as plain old common potatoes, which are in the *solanaceae* or nightshade family — good to know if you need to restrict nightshades in your diet. Sweet potatoes make the most incredibly delicious mash, and can be used in any way you would the common potato: in soups, roasted, mashed, made into fries or baked and stuffed with delicious accoutrements. In order to absorb all of the wonderful vitamin A stored in sweet potatoes, ensure you eat them with an element of fat (like coconut oil in mashed potatoes, or roasted in olive oil), as vitamin A is a fat-soluble vitamin which needs fat for proper absorption.

VERY SIMPLE SPANISH OMELETTE

2 teaspoons coconut oil

2 eggs

⅛–¼ sweet potato, washed and grated

¼ onion, chopped

½ teaspoon powdered garlic, plus other seasonings, to taste — chilli flakes, sea salt and pepper are great

optional: ¼ avocado, and lemon juice to serve

MAKES 1 LARGE OMELETTE

Pop a small frying pan on the stove over a medium heat (not too hot!), add the coconut oil and melt it. In a bowl, crack the eggs and whisk with a fork until just mixed. Add the sweet potato, onion, powdered garlic and other seasonings. Pour the egg mixture into the pan and leave to cook on low to medium heat, being careful not to let the bottom burn.

When the omelette is halfway cooked through, place the pan under a hot grill (broiler) for a minute or two to cook the top (be very aware to not put plastic pan handles under the grill, and equally as careful not to touch a metal handle with bare hands).

Gently slide the omelette from the pan and onto a serving plate. Enjoy hot with a little sliced avocado and freshly squeezed lemon on top.

4.

Legumes

Most plant-based protein sources are not complete, meaning they lack one or more of an essential amino acid that makes up a complete protein source for the body (most animal sources contain all twenty amino acids in sufficient quantity). By combining different kinds of plant-based protein sources, you can create a complete protein source — for example by having some gorgeous, nourishing wholesome lentil dahl with a side of brown and wild rice, or a handful of nuts in a salad with chickpeas (garbanzo beans). Legumes are an incredibly important part of the vegetarian diet for this reason, but other reasons are that they are filling, nourishing, versatile and dang delicious.

CHICKPEAS (GARBANZO BEANS)

We have a lot to be thankful to chickpeas for. They are the basis for hummus and falafel, *and* they help us manage weight and diabetes while promoting great digestion and preventing heart disease. A lot of great work for this tiny, valuable little legume.

Chickpeas are quite nutritionally balanced, as they combine important plant-based protein with lots of fibre and carbohydrate. Their protein (especially important for vegans and vegetarians) promotes lots of different functions in the body, including maintaining muscle mass, increasing satiety, assisting brain function and healthy skin and hair. And their fibre boosts the body's detoxification process by cleaning out the digestive tract and feeding beneficial bacteria colonies to increase nutrient absorption. Their carbohydrates also contribute to a well-functioning brain, and they fill the belly to ward off disordered eating patterns and fill up glycogen stores to prevent muscle wastage after exercise.

Chickpeas contain the antioxidant manganese for healthy joints; folate for healthy preconception (for both mum and dad), pregnancy and energy support; iron for healthy red blood cells and therefore energy production; and zinc for immunity, reproductive health and gorgeous skin.

It's incredibly easy to incorporate chickpeas regularly into your diet: they're perfect in salads, pan-fried or roasted, or as a dip (hummus), though they do require soaking and rinsing before use, just like all other legumes.

HARISSA CHICKPEAS (GARBANZO BEANS)

FOR ROUGHLY 1 CUP OF HARISSA PASTE:

1 red capsicum (pepper)

1 tablespoon coriander seeds

1 tablespoon caraway seeds

2 teaspoons cumin seeds

3 cloves garlic, peeled and roughly chopped

1 small onion, peeled and roughly chopped

5 red chillies (chili peppers)

2 tablespoons extra virgin olive oil

2 tablespoons lemon juice (or the juice from ½ a lemon)

sea salt and pepper, to taste

CHICKPEAS

1 x 400 g (14 oz) can chickpeas (garbanzo beans), drained and rinsed

coconut oil or extra virgin olive oil, to sauté

This recipe delivers hot and spicy vegan chickpea goodness that can be served on a bed of baby spinach or rocket (arugula), chopped cucumber with avocado, mint and coriander (cilantro) leaves, or with a tablespoon of full-fat natural yoghurt for the dairy tolerant amongst us!

The harissa paste also works fabulously as a marinade for chicken, fish or roasted vegetables if you enjoy chilli.

MAKES 3–4 SERVES

First, make the harissa paste. Place the capsicum under a hot grill (broiler) until the skin blackens and blisters. Remove and place in a bowl or container, cover in plastic wrap and put to one side. Once the capsicum has cooled, remove the skin, stem and seeds.

Place a frying pan over a low heat, then add the coriander, caraway and cumin seeds and dry toast, shaking the pan vigorously to avoid burning. Remove the seeds, place in a mortar and pestle or food processor, and grind or process to a powder.

Place the frying pan back onto a medium to high heat then add the garlic, onion and chillies and sauté until they begin to brown. Remove from the heat and transfer to a food processor, then add all the other ingredients (except the chickpeas and coconut oil) and blend until a paste forms. Taste and adjust seasoning if necessary.

Place 2 to 3 tablespoons of harissa paste into a bowl and add the chickpeas, stirring to coat them in the paste. Heat a little coconut oil in another frying pan, add the coated chickpeas and cook for 4 to 5 minutes until the chickpeas become a little crunchy.

Be very careful not to touch your nose or eyes after handling the chilli!

the benefits

*good source of
plant-based
protein*

❋

cardio-protective

❋

aid digestive health

BEANS

Here, beans have been lumped into the one category; however, there are many varieties, readily available for a range of uses, like cannellini beans, kidney beans, navy beans and black beans. All are different, and all are incredibly *tasty*. And wholesome. And nutritious!

I adore beans for really 'filling out' a recipe; they keep the belly nice and full thanks to their all-important protein. And their fantastic fibre, which feeds the good bacteria colonies of our gut, acts as an intestinal broom, cleaning out the digestive tract, keeping bowel movements regular and helping to prevent bowel cancer. This fibre also removes toxins from the colon (where they can be re-absorbed, if bowel movements aren't regular) and helps to lower cholesterol.

Easily cultivated, beans are part of the staple diet of many different cultures. They are full of fabulous nutrients like manganese, copper, B vitamins thiamine (B1) and folate (B9), phosphorous, magnesium and protein. These lovely legumes are an excellent choice for anyone at risk of heart disease, as they have been found to reduce cholesterol levels. They are also good for anyone suffering from or at risk of diabetes, thanks to their blood sugar-regulation properties.

Beans have developed an unfortunate reputation for causing flatulence, but it doesn't have to be that way! In order to reduce bean-related flatulence, the key is to prepare your beans properly. Ensure you soak your beans, preferably overnight, and rinse well to help remove the oligosaccharides, which are responsible for the extra gas production.

REFRIED BEANS

coconut oil

1 x 400 g (14 oz) cannellini beans or kidney beans, drained and rinsed

1 clove garlic, peeled and finely grated

sea salt and pepper, to taste

juice of 1 lemon or lime

½–1 teaspoon chilli flakes

extra virgin olive oil, to serve

Refried Beans are the perfect accompaniment to Mexican food or can be used as a dip.

MAKES ENOUGH FOR 4 AS A SIDE
OR IN A TACO

Place a small frying pan over medium to high heat and add a little coconut oil; then add the beans. Stir until the beans are coated in coconut oil, then add the garlic. Keep stirring until the beans start to become slightly crunchy, then mash them roughly with a fork right there in the pan. Add a little extra coconut oil if necessary.

Remove from the heat, and while still warm, mix through the lemon or lime juice and chilli flakes, and season liberally with salt and pepper.

the benefits

digestive health

❋

weight management

❋

good source of
plant-based protein

❋

energy production

LENTILS

Lentils are an important staple food for millions of people throughout the world. They are an especially important element in the diets of vegans and vegetarians as a source of protein, and beneficial for anyone suffering with constipation, because these little round things are absolutely riddled with fibre and are guaranteed to get things moving!

When cooked properly, I find lentils to be the most wonderfully belly-filling, nourishing comfort food, and they can be used to convert lots of meat-filled dishes into vegetarian, such as burgers, casseroles and Vegetarian Shepherd's Pie (see p. 54). These gorgeous little legumes have a good amount of vital nutrients too, like potassium, molybdenum (which assists with enzymatic activities like the breaking down of protein), zinc, calcium, the aforementioned all-important fibre, some B vitamins, protein, iron, copper and manganese.

Lentils are wonderful to include in your diet if you are trying to manage your weight, suffer from digestive complaints (although going from no lentils to all lentils can cause an upset tummy too; introduce them little by little into your diet, and ensure they are rinsed and cooked correctly) or have high cholesterol, as all that fibre gives the liver a helping hand with the detoxification process.

Cooked, cold lentils are a lovely way to fill out a salad, and especially lovely as the base for a warming bowl of Wholesome Lentil Dahl.

WHOLESOME LENTIL DAHL

6 teaspoons coriander
seeds

6 teaspoons cumin seeds

4 teaspoons chilli flakes
or chopped red chilli
(chili pepper)

4 teaspoons garam masala

4 teaspoons turmeric
powder

2 tablespoons coconut oil

1 onion, chopped

1 whole bulb of garlic
(not just a clove, a bulb!),
peeled and chopped

½ bunch coriander
(cilantro), stalks and leaves
chopped separately

1 knob ginger, peeled and
finely chopped

½ medium pumpkin
(winter squash) or approx.
3–4 cups cubed

2 x 400 g (14 oz) cans
lentils, drained and rinsed

2 tomatoes, chopped

5 cups filtered water or
good quality vegetable
stock

optional: coconut cream,
kefir or full-fat natural
yoghurt, to serve

SERVES 6–8

Dry toast the coriander seeds, cumin seeds, chilli, garam masala and turmeric powder in a frying pan until warm and fragrant (the coriander seeds might 'pop'). Shake the pan constantly to prevent burning. Transfer to a mortar and pestle, or use a stick blender or food processor, and grind to form a well combined powder. Take a moment to deeply inhale the gorgeous, exotic scent of your dahl spice mix. Leave this mix to one side for the moment.

Add the coconut oil to a large pot and place on a medium to high heat. Then add the onion, garlic, chopped coriander (stalks only) and ginger, and sauté, stirring until well combined and ever so gently browned. Add the ground spices and stir through well. You may need to incrementally add a little more coconut oil. Now add the pumpkin, lentils and tomato, again stirring until well combined and the pumpkin and tomato have softened slightly. Add the water or stock one cup at a time, stirring through until the pumpkin and lentils are covered, stirring at a high heat until boiling. As soon as boiling point is reached, reduce heat to a low simmer, cover the pot and allow to simmer for at least 30 minutes or until the pumpkin is well cooked through.

Serve the dahl alone or with wild or brown rice or quinoa (or a combination of those), or Cauliflower Rice (see p. 30), then top with a tablespoon of either coconut cream, kefir or full-fat natural yoghurt, and of lots of chilli (chili peppers) and coriander leaves. This dish is absolutely wonderful soul food and is deliciously warming and immune-boosting (thanks to the massive garlic dose as well as plenty of vitamin A precursors) when fighting a cold or flu.

the benefits

antioxidant

❊

cancer protective

❊

cardio-protective

❊

energy production

❊

skin health

GREEN BEANS

Humble and green and nutritionally mighty, green beans (or string beans) are a long and lovely bean dream. When fresh, they make the most satisfying *snap* when snapped in half, and the most nutrient-dense and delicious beans should be bright green and firm, not floppy.

While steamed green beans have forever been a mainstay of the 'meat and three veg' culture, there are numerous ways to cook these guys to shake things up and get them into your diet as much as possible. You can pan-fry them in coconut oil and spices, roast them, serve them raw as dipping implements for hummus, blanch them and serve cold, or chop into short lengths and pop into a lovely curry or stir-fry.

Green beans are all business when it comes to nutrient content: they contain a wealth of antioxidants and eye-protective carotenoids; flavonoids like the impressive quercetin, kaempferol (which inhibits the development of cancer cells, and is cardio-protective, reducing the hardening of the arteries) and catechins (also cardio-protective and helpful in weight management); and a long, long list of vitamins, minerals and other micronutrients like vitamin K, manganese, fibre, B-group vitamins, magnesium, vitamin C, calcium, chromium, iron, omega-3 fatty acids, potassium, choline, protein and vitamin E.

THAI BEAN SALAD

5–6 handfuls green beans, topped and tailed

⅓ cup coconut milk

2 red chillies (chili peppers)

1 cup basil leaves

1 cup mint leaves

juice of 1 lime

3 ripe tomatoes, cut into quarters

1 Lebanese (short) cucumber, cut into diagonal slices

¼ onion, chopped

½ red onion, sliced thinly

¾ cup raw almonds, chopped

SERVES 4

Bring a medium saucepan of water to the boil. Drop the beans into the boiling water and blanch for 2 to 3 minutes. They should be bright green and still crunchy. Drain and rinse in cold water, then set aside.

In a food processor, combine the coconut milk, chillies, basil, mint, onion and lime juice. Blend until a smooth paste is formed.

In a large serving bowl, toss together the beans, sliced tomatoes and cucumbers. Then add the paste and gently stir through, and top with red onion and almonds.

5.

OTHER
Vegetables

These vegetables don't belong in the other categories, but are vitally important all the same. Mushrooms aren't even technically a plant! But each and every one of them is a worthy inclusion for their awesome nutrient profiles. There are traditional staples like tomatoes (technically a fruit, but they're used like a vegetable and I can't fathom the Mediterranean diet without them), zucchinis (courgettes) and pumpkins (winter squash), and the not so traditional but wildly nutrient-rich like sprouts, which are the itty bitty form of the plant when it is at its most health-giving. All of these vegetables are user-friendly, widely available, taste amazing and are fantastic for maintaining great health.

TOMATO

There is a philosophy in Chinese medicine that a food resembling a particular human organ is what is best to eat in order to keep that organ healthy. If this is true, then surely the tomato is one of the most convincing forms of evidence to support this. Just like a human heart, the tomato has four chambers (in which it houses its seeds), and these beautiful summer fruits contain many, many important nutrients vital for heart health.

Perhaps the most important of those nutrients is the carotenoid lycopene, which is powerfully cardio-protective, lowing total cholesterol levels as well as LDL cholesterol (the 'bad' cholesterol) and reducing triglyceride levels in the blood. Lycopene also helps to prevent atherosclerosis (hardening of the arteries) and is increased in availability and most abundant in *cooked* tomatoes. So the cooking process will get plenty of lycopene goodness for your body to use up! Lycopene is also strongly indicated as a cancer-protective force of nature, and has been most studied for its effectiveness against prostate cancer. Lycopene is a great inclusion in the diet of anyone at risk of this insidious tumour. Lycopene has also been indicated in various studies against lung and stomach cancers.

In conjunction with lycopene, tomatoes also house antioxidant phytonutrients like rutin (an anti-inflammatory, pain-relieving flavonol that also contributes to healthy blood vessels), kaempferol (antibacterial, anti-inflammatory, cancer-hating but heart-loving neuroprotective wonder compound) and lutein (an essential nutrient for eye health to prevent age-related degenerative eye diseases like macular degeneration) amongst a ton of other nutrients. Aside from this, tomatoes also dole out vitamin C, vitamin K, potassium, copper, fibre, vitamin A precursors, manganese, B vitamins, magnesium, vitamin E, iron, zinc and a little protein.

Tomatoes are extremely easy to grow in warm climates. They don't require a lot of TLC and the heirloom varieties will self-seed providing many years of plentiful tomatoes.

SPANISH BAKED EGGS

coconut oil or extra virgin olive oil

2 large ripe tomatoes, chopped and sprinkled with a little sea salt

½ cup finely chopped capsicum (pepper)

corn kernels from 1 fresh corn cob carefully removed with a sharp knife

2 cloves garlic, peeled and crushed, plus 2 teaspoons powdered garlic

squeeze of lemon juice

1 teaspoon chilli flakes *or* freshly chopped chilli (chili pepper)

1 teaspoon smoked paprika

4 eggs, at room temperature

1 cup cooked quinoa

200 g (7 oz) cooked kidney beans, drained and rinsed

optional: ½ avocado, chopped parsley or basil and a bed of rocket (arugula), to serve, plus extra wedges of lemon

SERVES 2 VERY HUNGRY PEOPLE

Preheat the oven to 180°C (350°F). Place an ovenproof frying pan a medium to high heat and add a little oil. Add the tomatoes, capsicum, corn and garlic, and as it cooks add a big squeeze of lemon juice. This will encourage the tomatoes to cook through and brown a little. Now turn the heat down to low to medium, add the chilli and paprika and stir. Add beans and quinoa and stir until ingredients are well combined.

Take the pan off the heat and using the back of a tablespoon or similar-sized utensil, form four little divots in the tomato mix, each large enough to contain an egg, but not through to the base of the pan. Crack one egg into each divot, and place back onto a gentle heat to cook for 5 minutes.

Place the whole pan in the oven (make sure your pan is ovenproof, or else place the pan only (not the handle) under the grill (broiler) on a low heat) and allow to cook for 10 to 20 minutes. Ideally, the eggs will cook but will be runny inside. This creates a glorious richness in the tomato base as you eat it.

Once cooked, take extreme care removing the pan from the oven as the handle will be extremely hot (I use an oven mitt as well as a tea towel around the handle). Arrange a bed of fresh rocket (arugula) on two serving plates, then use a large serving spoon to spoon the mixture onto the plates. Serve topped with a little avocado and a squeeze of lemon juice.

the benefits

liver detoxification

✳

healthy bones

✳

digestive health

✳

energy production

✳

*source of plant-based
protein*

SPROUTS

'Sprouts' is the generic term given to any type of germinated nut, bean or seed; it describes that magical moment when the little green shoot starts to poke out of the seed, when a tiny plant life is beginning. This is kicked off by a series of seemingly magical chemical processes that result in a plant food that is at its most nutrient dense, and those nutrients are at their most available to your body.

The nutrient power punch in sprouts is a welcome leg-up for everyone nutritionally, but is especially fantastic for vegans and vegetarians and others on restricted diets, who sometimes can struggle with bioavailability (the nutrient's ability to be absorbed and utilized by the body) of some plant-based nutrients. Sprouts contain an incredible array of nutrients like proteins, omega-3 fatty acids, vitamin K, fibre, vitamin C, B-group vitamins, vitamin A precursors, manganese, zinc, iron, magnesium and absorbable calcium. They also contain enzymes that help to break down our food and further absorb nutrients. How very nice of them.

Thanks to that extra-long résumé of nutrients, sprouts are indicated in the management of virtually any disorder you could throw them at. A little sprout action added to your diet makes a world of difference to overall health, and they are incredibly simple to make at home. Broccoli sprouts are especially wonderful for any liver and detoxification related issue, including hormonal imbalance. Once germinated, seeds, nuts and beans taste wildly different, from ultra spicy and peppery to mild and nutty, so get your experimenting hat on and try sprouting all sorts of seeds, wholegrains and legumes!

DIY SPROUTS

YOU WILL NEED

Sprouting apparatus. This can be a specialized sprouting kit, purchased cheaply online or from most health food stores, or improvised with materials at home. The only restriction is that the container should be opaque (so not glass) and shouldn't be wooden or metal. Ceramic, china and enamel containers are great.

A strainer. This can be muslin (cheesecloth), a strainer, or colander for beans (some seeds and legumes might wash straight through a colander)

paper towel or muslin (cheesecloth)

½ cup of your chosen nut, seed or legume. Experiment with dried beans and seeds. Favourites include broccoli seeds, rocket (arugula) seeds (these create an extraordinary peppery taste), watercress, quinoa, mustard seeds, mung beans, lentils and chickpeas (garbanzo beans). You can buy organic, non-GMO growers' seeds easily online.

Sprouts are a fabulous way to not only add taste and textural interest to a meal, but they will also nutritionally supercharge it, and it's incredibly easy to make your own sprouts.

HOW TO SPROUT

Rinse your legumes or seeds thoroughly to get rid of any dust and impurities, then soak overnight in tepid water. In the morning, strain the little darlings and rinse thoroughly once more. Now, you might need to remove any legumes or seeds that are floating on the surface, as these guys won't play the game and sprout.

Drain off the water, rinse and place in your chosen receptacle. Cover with a few sheets of damp paper towel or muslin. You want a nice damp environment, but they should not be sitting in water. Place in a cool, dark area for 8 hours.

After 8 hours, cover the sprouts in water, let them sit for 5 minutes, then drain and again place in a cool, dark area. Repeat this process twice daily, covering in damp paper towel or muslin each time, until your legumes or seeds have sprouted. As they germinate, the outer husks and shells of the seed or legume with soften and fall off. This is fine; allow these to drain away.

Depending on your chosen crop, the seeds should germinate within three to five days (rocket/arugula will shoot within 24 to 48 hours, whereas chickpeas might take five or six days).

Eat on their own, or as a wonderful addition to a salad.

the benefits

energy production

✳

immune function

✳

skin health

✳

reproductive health

ZUCCHINI (COURGETTES)

Zucchini vary greatly in taste according to their size, from the slightly bitter and enormous variegated varieties to the sweet, small, dark green young zucchini. Though subtle in flavour, this staple of Mediterranean cooking contains a long list of essential nutrients like manganese, vitamin C, magnesium, fibre, potassium, lots of B-group vitamins, zinc, omega-3 fatty acids, calcium, iron, choline and a little protein. With a contents list like that it's hard to narrow down the huge range of health conditions that a regular zucchini wouldn't do wonders for, but it's safe to say these easy-to-grow green machines are fantastic for heart health thanks to their fibre, magnesium, omega-3 and potassium; brain, skin and immunity benefits thanks to their zinc, vitamin C and omega-3 fatty acids; and they are anti-inflammatory and antioxidant to boot.

That subtle flavour profile is precisely what makes zucchini such a regular in my kitchen; they are incredibly versatile and lend themselves to an infinite number of dishes, from soup to casseroles to zucchini bread. You can even stuff and fry the bright yellow zucchini flowers (found at specialty grocery stores or growers'/farmers' markets). As a part of a gluten-free diet they are the crowning glory amongst vegetables as they replace pasta when spiralized, as in the recipe on page 11.

STUFFED ZUCCHINI
(COURGETTES)

300 g (10½ oz) beef or lamb mince (vegetarians can substitute grated carrot or leave out)

3–4 garlic cloves, peeled and sliced

½ red capsicum (pepper), finely chopped, seeds removed

1 small onion, chopped

2 large ripe tomatoes, chopped

¾ cup cooked quinoa

2 large zucchini (courgettes), halved lengthways and seeds scraped out

1 egg

thyme leaves, finely chopped

spring onions (scallions) chopped, and chilli flakes, to serve

My favourite way to eat zucchini is simply steamed, with thinly sliced garlic in the mix, and finished with a tiny bit of olive oil, salt and pepper. Seriously. I'm not sure what wizardry the garlic performs but the end result is powerful and delicious, and I recommend you give it a try. Steamed zucchini on its own: frankly bland, 1 out of 10 stars. Steamed zucchini with garlic: 11 out of 10 stars. I get mid-week cravings for it all the time. I also don't mind consuming my zucchini in fritter form either, but the Greek half of me also loves them stuffed, as in the following recipe.

SERVES 4 AS A SIDE

Preheat the oven to 180°C (350°F). Place a large frying pan over a medium to high heat, then add the meat, garlic, capsicum, onion and tomatoes. Stir until the meat is browned and vegetables are cooked through, then add the quinoa and stir. Transfer to a bowl and allow to cool slightly.

Line a baking tray (baking sheet) with baking (parchment) paper or foil, then place the zucchini halves onto the tray, hollowed-side up.

In a small bowl, lightly beat the egg then stir it through the semi-cooled filling. Spoon the filling into the zucchini halves. Bake in the oven for approximately 20 to 30 minutes, or until zucchini are completely cooked. Sprinkle over the chopped spring onions and chilli flakes.

PUMPKIN (WINTER SQUASH)

Pumpkins are divine both sweet (in spiced pumpkin pie) or savoury (in Thai pumpkin soup) and any way you eat them, you're giving yourself a gorgeous range of nutrients. Pumpkins include a massive dose of vitamin K, a range of B-group vitamins, potassium, copper, magnesium, iron, manganese, phosphorous and zinc, as well as lutein and zeaxanthin, powerful antioxidants which prevent age-related degeneration of the eye like macular degeneration. Pumpkins contain nutrients essential for a great immune system and glowing skin, like vitamins C, A and E and zinc, as well as copper and energy-promoting iron. The beautiful orange flesh also contains lots of fibre to promote good digestion and weight management. Pumpkins are deliciously sweet, and although they contain natural sugars, they are still great for diabetics to satisfy a sweet tooth as they contain a lot of water and fibre to go with the sweetness and won't disrupt blood sugar levels too drastically.

Related to cucumbers and zucchini (courgettes), pumpkins are relatively easy to grow with a high yield if you have the room; they do like space as they are a ground-covering vine. The seeds of the pumpkin contain their own range of incredible nutrients, so don't discard them when you go about cutting up your pumpkin! Read all about the nutritious goodness of pumpkin seeds (pepitas) on page 135.

COMFORT SALAD

½ small pumpkin (winter squash) *or* 1 butternut pumpkin (squash)

2 teaspoons coconut oil, melted

½ cup walnuts

1 pear, washed and grated

2 cups chicory (witlof/ Belgian endive), finely sliced (if endive isn't available you can use another leafy green, such as rocket/arugula)

1 x 400 g (14 oz) can chickpeas (garbanzo beans), drained and rinsed

½ avocado

goat's cheese, to serve

sesame oil, to serve

SERVES 2

Preheat the oven to 180°C (350°F). Cut your pumpkin into quarters or halves and remove the membrane and seeds (keep the seeds and roast separately if you wish). Lightly rub the coconut oil all over the pumpkin, and bake the pumpkin for around 30 minutes or until cooked through. This shall be your salad 'bowl'.

In a separate bowl, assemble all other ingredients except for the goat's cheese and sesame oil. Place the mixed salad ingredients inside your pumpkin bowl then top with crumbled goat's cheese and a sprinkle of sesame oil.

the benefits

skin health

✻

reproductive health

✻

immune function

✻

brain function

AVOCADO

Avocados! What a powerful and wondrous fruit! They are one of my top ten foods of all time, purely based on taste. They make everything *better*. They're also little round bombs of nutrients, packed with heaps of vitamin K, vitamin C, various B-group vitamins (including B9, B6, B5, B1, B2 and B3) potassium and vitamin E.

Regularly including avocados in your diet can improve your skin, regulate blood pressure, reduce inflammatory markers and help to manage weight. As a high-fat food, a little avocado in a meal will increase satiety (help you to feel fuller for longer) which helps to curb cravings for bad (trans) fats and high-sugar foods. It is also high in fibre, and many, many studies have shown that increasing fibre in the diet is key for weight loss. The humble avocado's fat is mainly oleic acid, which is the same fat component that makes olive oil a champion of heart health. It is anti-inflammatory, and has been shown to lower cholesterol and triglyceride levels and regulate blood pressure (can you hear me, diabetics of this world?).

Another vital factor in avocado's superstardom is the fact that it helps you absorb some really important fat-soluble antioxidant vitamins such as vitamins A, D, E and K that are only absorbed in the presence of fat. Avocado also contains lutein, which is crucial for long-term eye health, warding off the development of cataracts and macular degeneration.

Last but not least, I generally like to recommend avocados to anyone struggling with hormone regulation and fertility issues, as they contain those wonderful fats that are required for the production of sex and fertility hormones in both men and women.

CHOCOLATE AVOCADO MOUSSE

2 ripe avocados (If they're overripe, save them for guacamole. If they're not ripe enough, pop them in a paper bag with a ripe banana. Bananas excrete a natural chemical that will ripen a hard avocado in a day.)

½ vanilla bean, seeds removed

½ cup maple syrup

½ cup cacao powder

optional: ½ teaspoon mixed cinnamon and nutmeg *or* small pinch of salt, plus ½ cup coconut milk if the mousse is too 'dark chocolate' for your liking

The day I discovered this miracle of human invention I was quite perturbed by the thought of eating avocado as a dessert. To my mind, this was incorrect, an assault on the palate, an injustice to the saintly avocado.

Luckily I am driven by a pathological desire for new ways to make desserts healthy, so I gave it a go and have never looked back. You can add a couple tablespoons of melted coconut oil or cocoa butter to the mix to turn this into a gorgeous ganache-like icing (frosting) for cakes and brownies, that firms up when chilled. Or do as I do, and eat it straight from the bowl.

MAKES 4–6 SERVINGS

Place all ingredients in a food processor and blend thoroughly. I say thoroughly but I actually mean extremely thoroughly. Blend for at least a few minutes, because goodness help you if there is a chunk of unblended avocado floating in the mix when you taste it, and the longer it is blended, the lighter the mixture becomes. Add a little coconut milk if it is too rich or too dark.

Spoon into four or six individual cups or glasses, then place them in the fridge and allow to chill for at least 2 hours.

CAPSICUM (PEPPER)

In my humble opinion, red capsicums are one of the finest raw foods to eat. Which is great because as it turns out, that's the best way to eat them! These beautiful, colourful globes of yum provide sweet flavour and crunchy texture to salads, are great cooked on the barbecue or cut into sticks as a dipping implement or on their own as a snack. They are to die for when stuffed with quinoa and lots of garlic in a tomato-based sauce. I just plain eat them like an apple on a regular basis.

When eaten raw, a glossy, ripe red capsicum deals out an enormous quantity of vitamin C, as well as various carotenoids, B-group vitamins, fibre, vitamin E, potassium, vitamin K, phosphorous and magnesium. This good mix of nutrients — as well as their wonderful array of phytonutrients like quercetin, hesperidin (for brain function and a nicely pumping circulatory system), ferulic acid (a *big* anti-ageing skin phytonutrient) and luteolin (anti-ageing, cognitive function and brain health) — means capsicums are highly antioxidant, anti-ageing, anti-inflammatory handfuls of greatness.

Do not despair if people point and laugh at you, like they do me, when I am out and about chowing down on a whole capsicum; when you're at a ripe old age, in perfect health and looking twenty years younger from all that capsicum eating, you'll be laughing right back!

SUPER SEED
ANTIOXIDANT SALAD

¼ red cabbage, finely chopped

2 large carrots, washed and grated

½ pear, washed and grated

½ large raw beetroot, washed and grated

½ red onion, sliced

½ red capsicum (pepper), de-seeded, finely sliced

optional: 1 tablespoon very finely chopped ginger

½ cup sunflower seeds

½ cup linseeds/flaxseeds

½ cup sesame seeds

extra virgin olive oil (the best you can afford) and unfiltered apple cider vinegar, to dress

I make an enormous bowl of this salad and keep it in the fridge so I can stick a big handful on top of some fresh greens and rocket (arugula) from the garden for lunch. It lasts forever and is delicious and satisfying, and contains a glorious spectrum of nutrients, including a little protein, fibre, vitamins A, C and E (plus the essential element of fat in order to absorb the fat-soluble vitamins A and E), a little B vitamin action and a bunch of minerals. It's a fantastic blood and liver cleansing salad mix too, is anti-inflammatory and if you dress it with apple cider vinegar it's going to increase your hydrochloric (stomach) acid production and help overall digestion.

SERVES 4 AS A MAIN MEAL

Combine all ingredients in a large bowl, except the olive oil and vinegar. Add a little oil and vinegar then toss gently to combine. Serve on top of rocket (arugula) and/or leafy greens.

Hot tip: grate the cabbage, carrots, pear and beetroot straight into the serving bowl or chop in a food processor to save time and washing up!

EGGPLANT (AUBERGINE)

Eggplants (aubergines) are the deep purple fleshy member of the nightshade family (along with tomatoes, potatoes, capsicums/peppers etc.) that is instantly recognizable from Mediterranean, Chinese, Indian and Middle Eastern cooking (as well as, you know, its bizarre shape and insanely gorgeous hue).

Eggplants are *big* on fibre, and also contain vitamin K, B-group vitamins, manganese and potassium, as well as some incredible phytonutrients including chlorogenic acid (an incredibly powerful antioxidant that has also been shown to lower blood pressure) and nasunin, another highly antioxidant compound particularly protective of brain cells and their functions.

This gorgeous vegetable is very easy to grow at home, even in a pot, and requires similar conditions to its tomato and capsicum (pepper) cousins. Vegetables within the nightshade family can exacerbate arthritic pain, so limit these if you suffer from arthritis, including rheumatoid arthritis.

Eggplant lends a luscious creaminess to the Middle Eastern baba ganoush dip (it's just plain fun to say, but is delicious with Flax Crackers on page 133) or fried in a little coconut oil and drizzled with tahini dressing, as in the recipe on the opposite page.

PAN-FRIED EGGPLANT (AUBERGINE) WITH TAHINI DRESSING

1 eggplant (aubergine),
cut lengthways into 1 cm
(⅓ in.) thick slices

coconut oil

sea salt and pepper, to
taste, plus chilli (chili
pepper) or smoked
paprika if desired

DRESSING

¼ cup water

¼ cup tahini

⅛ cup organic unfiltered
apple cider vinegar
(or lemon juice)

1 heaped teaspoon
garlic powder

sea salt and pepper, to taste

SERVES 4 AS A SIDE

Place all dressing ingredients in a jar; tightly screw on the lid and shake the jar vigorously, like you're Peter Allen at a maraca convention, until the ingredients are well combined then set aside.

Heat a little coconut oil in a frying pan on a high heat. Place the eggplant strips in the pan, ensuring they are well coated in oil (move the strips about in the pan). Fry for a few minutes, turning once to cook the other side. Once all the strips are golden brown and cooked through, remove from the pan, place onto serving plates and drizzle over the dressing. Season while still warm.

the benefits

cancer protective

✳

energy production

✳

hormone balance

✳

*fantastic for vegan and
vegetarians*

MUSHROOMS

Mushrooms are bizarre and fascinating and mysterious,
and I want to become a mycologist immediately. The health
implications of these weird organisms (they're not plants!
Nor are they animals!) are enormous, with emerging research coming out all the time to
declare their latest magical superpower.

For a long time now, mushrooms have been known as 'vegan meat' not just because
the large field varieties are already very helpfully shaped like a burger, but because they
contain vitamins that vegans will struggle to source outside of meat products, particularly B
vitamins like B12, which takes a long time to show up with deficiency symptoms.

Mushrooms contain conjugated linoleic acid, which is a fatty acid that helps to reduce
the overproduction of estrogen in estrogen-dominant women (it can happen to men,
too). This is extremely important as this overproduction can have wide ranging effects on
the body (such as weight gain and insulin resistance) and mental health (mood swings
and depression). It is also vitally important for reducing the risk of developing estrogen-
receptor-positive breast cancer, which is encouraged to grow larger in the presence of too

much estrogen. Studies have shown different kinds of mushroom extracts to be effective against other different kinds of cancer, too.

Mushrooms are not only going to town on cancer, but at the same time they're going to boost your immunity, reduce inflammation, provide a power blast of antioxidants as well as a bunch of other fantastic nutrients (especially for vegetarians!), like B vitamins (including B6, B9 and B12, which work synergistically — see 'The lowdown' below), copper, selenium, potassium, zinc, manganese, choline, protein and phosphorous.

I'm usually the first to jump on the foraging bandwagon, but following an unfortunate event where I ate the furry, revolting leaves of a false dandelion plant rather than an actual dandelion, I most definitely only recommend foraging for mushrooms with a certified expert who knows exactly what they're looking at; mushroom varieties can look very similar, but where one will be harmless, another will be deadly. Take an expert, or farm your own in a box under the kitchen sink with a pre-ordered box of soil impregnated with mushroom spores. That, or stay completely safe and buy from the growers' market!

THE LOWDOWN: B VITAMINS

B vitamins are incredibly important in isolation for a wide variety of health concerns, from cognitive function to energy production to preventing birth defects in the early stages of development. When taken in supplement form, B vitamins should always be taken as a 'complex'; in other words, packaged with other B vitamins. The reason for this is that some B vitamins work together with and rely on other B vitamins in order to work most effectively (particularly B6, B9 and B12) — that is, they work synergistically. The beauty of eating a wholefood diet is that you have the best chance of gaining a range of vitamins that need to be consumed together in order to work together, like the Bs.

CHICKEN, MUSHROOM AND GINGER HOTPOT

500 g (1 lb) chicken breast or thigh, skin removed, cut into 2 cm (⅔ in.) pieces

1 knob ginger (or more if you are keen on ginger), peeled and sliced thinly

1 onion, sliced thinly

3 cloves garlic, peeled and sliced thinly

2 tablespoons rice wine vinegar

1 cup chicken stock (homemade, or a good quality store-bought one without any nasty additives)

sea salt and pepper, to taste

¼ cup tamari

250 g (9 oz) large mushrooms, sliced thinly

sesame seeds and sesame oil, to serve

One-pot Wonder!

SERVES 4 HUNGRY PEOPLE

Preheat the oven to 180°C (350°F). Pop all the ingredients except the mushrooms in a medium-sized casserole dish with a lid (or make your own lid with foil). Place in the oven and cook for 70 minutes.

Remove the casserole dish from the oven and check that the chicken is cooked through. Then add the mushrooms, give everything a stir, and allow to cook for a further 20 minutes.

Once ready, spoon onto serving plates and top with sesame seeds and a small drizzle of sesame oil. Serve with ½ cup of quinoa or brown rice per person, and some Garlicky Greens (see p. 195).

ASPARAGUS

Asparagus, king amongst side dishes! It looks so lovely on the plate, as well as being nutritious and delicious. Besides its beautiful green colour, asparagus is a powerhouse of nutrients including fibre, vitamin C and vitamin B9, as well as vitamins A, E and K (these last three vitamins are fat soluble, meaning we only absorb them with an element of fat in the meal. I very lightly sauté asparagus in coconut oil then add sesame seeds. Easy — and it further increases the vitamin E and calcium content through the addition of lovely little sesame seeds.

Asparagus also contains chromium, the magical little mineral that is extremely important for diabetics and people with blood sugar issues, as it increases insulin's ability to transport sugar from the bloodstream into cells for energy. Asparagus also contains glutathione, the compound that helps our livers in phase 2 of detoxification. It is also full to the brim with antioxidants. Eat asparagus and your body gets rid of toxins, making it a super anti-ageing food. Last but not least, it contains asparagine, the amino acid that makes asparagus a mild diuretic. Basically it makes you wee more, and this, in conjunction with drinking lots and lots of water, will help reduce fluid retention.

Yes, it can be a little more expensive than some other vegetables, but please pick some up once or twice a week. It won't send you bankrupt, and its health and beautifying qualities are impressive!

LEMON MUSTARD GREEN SALAD WITH POACHED EGG

3 handfuls rocket (arugula)

6 asparagus spears, woody bottom part of the stalk removed

5 spring onions (scallions), sliced

1 cup mint leaves, tightly packed, finely sliced

¼ cup thyme, loosely packed, leaves roughly stripped from the twig and gently rubbed between the fingers

1 bulb fennel, leaves removed (save for garnish), bulb and stalks finely sliced

2 cups broad (fava) beans, shelled

2 eggs

1 cup raw walnuts

DRESSING

juice of 2 lemons (approx. 4 tablespoons)

4 tablespoons extra virgin olive oil

pepper, to taste

1 heaped tablespoon Dijon mustard

This is a variation on a recipe I stole from my big brother, which I have transformed to make it more everyday friendly.

I'm not going to lie to you: I am terrible at poaching eggs. But they add a richness to this salad that can't be recreated, so I definitely recommend that you practise and persist with the egg! This salad goes perfectly with all kinds of fish and meat, and is delicious and satisfying on its own. Some other green veg that would fit perfectly into this salad include peas, finely chopped cabbage, sautéed zucchini (courgettes), pan-fried brussels sprouts and beautiful young snow pea (mangetout) shoots.

SERVES 4

Spread a layer of rocket on the bottom of a large serving bowl. Place a saucepan with plenty of water over a high heat and bring to the boil. Add the asparagus and blanch for no more than 1 minute, remove from the saucepan, place in a colander and run under cold water. The spears should be tender but still crunchy.

Refill the saucepan and bring to the boil, add the broad beans. Cook until they float to the surface, remove to a colander and run under cold water for 30 seconds.

Poach the eggs. The most important part of poaching eggs is to use the freshest eggs available. Place another saucepan on the stove, fill to three-quarters with water and bring to the boil. Adding 2 tablespoons of white vinegar to the water can help to keep the egg whites together. Reduce to a low heat so that gentle bubbles pop to the surface of the water. Carefully crack your eggs into the water and leave them for 2 to 3 minutes, then remove with a slotted spoon.

Combine all dressing ingredients in a jar, screw on the lid and shake until well combined.

Add all other salad ingredients (apart from the eggs) on top of the rocket and toss to combine. Top with poached egg, the lacy little fennel leaves and the dressing.

6. Nuts & SEEDS

Nuts and seeds are our phenomenal good-fat and protein-rich friends of the plant universe who make a perfect, delicious and energy-sustaining snack that keeps you feeling full and happy (seriously happy; walnuts have always helped me kick the blues).

Nuts and seeds play a pivotal role in almost every traditional cuisine the world over. They impart texture, flavour, nutrients and richness to all kinds of dishes, including savoury, sweet and spicy. And, perhaps most importantly, they create the most delicious and healthy alternative to traditional ingredients for pastries and desserts: they can be used as pie crusts, cheesecake base *and* filling, and as the filling main ingredient in loaves and *tortas*.

the benefits

cardio-protective

*

immune boosting

*

antifungal, antibacterial, antiviral

*

promotes oral health

*

assists brain health

*

healthy skin

*

healthy metabolism

COCONUT

Coconuts have been on the fad-food radar for a while now. Fortunately, this rotund giant of the seed world lives up to the hype. Coconuts taste *amazing*. They're sweet and they're fatty and everything human taste buds seek out. Luckily they also pack a load of helpful nutrients, which makes me throw my hands up in exaltation because coconuts taste like dessert but are good for you (dreams can come true).

These marvellous things contain lauric acid, a fatty acid that is antifungal, antibacterial and antiviral. A teaspoon of coconut oil in a cup of herbal tea is wonderfully soothing while beneficial for whatever ails you. Coconut oil is also a lovely skin moisturizer, even for oily and acne-prone skins (it's all I use).

Coconuts are cardio-protective, as they are effective in balancing good and bad cholesterol ratios and reducing triglycerides in the blood. They are also wonderful for diabetics, as coconut slows down the release of sugar into the bloodstream. The fats in coconut are medium-chain triglycerides which, when consumed, completely bypass the gallbladder and are directly metabolized by the liver into energy. This produces fat-burning ketone bodies, which increase the body's ability to burn fat, particularly harmful abdominal fat. These ketone bodies have also been indicated in the management of Alzheimer's disease and have been shown to be effective in reducing the duration and frequency of seizures in some epileptic children.

All hail our hairy little friend of the plant kingdom!

CHIMPDAD'S GENUINE SRI LANKAN FISH CURRY

Chimpdad is my beloved stepdad. He has long, lanky limbs just like a chimpanzee and lives near the ocean on the Western Australian coast, and has access to the greatest seafood on earth. My idea of a wonderful day is to go out prawning (catching shrimp) with him and my sister in the baking hot sun. There is something extremely satisfying about going out and catching your own dinner. We never catch more than we need, though. While this recipe uses fish, prawns (shrimp) would work fine, too; if you use them, just be sure to devein them properly (that 'vein' doesn't hold blood ...). However, if you're making this to the letter be sure to choose a sustainably caught, firm-fleshed, white fish that won't disintegrate in the mix. Ask your fishmonger what is the freshest, sustainably caught, and best for curry-making.

SERVES 4
NOTE: THIS RECIPE REQUIRES SOAKING TIME

SRI LANKAN CURRY POWDER

6 tablespoons coriander seeds

2 tablespoons cumin seeds

1 teaspoons fennel seeds

1 teaspoons mustard seeds

2 tablespoons cinnamon

4 cloves

4 cardamom pods

5 dried curry leaves

1 teaspoon whole black peppercorns

FISH CURRY

1 medium-sized sweet potato, cut into 2 cm (⅔ in.) cubes

3 tablespoons coconut oil or ghee

1 red onion, peeled and finely chopped

6 cloves garlic, peeled and finely chopped

2 tablespoons Sri Lankan curry powder

1 teaspoons turmeric

1 teaspoon chilli flakes

400 ml (13½ fl oz) coconut milk

1 large knob ginger, finely grated

1 tablespoon cinnamon

20 curry leaves

juice of 1 lime

1 tablespoon fish sauce

sea salt and pepper, to taste

600 g (1⅓ lb) firm white fish (e.g. mackerel, trevally or similar), cut into 2.5 cm (1 in.) cubes, covered in milk and stored in refrigerator for at least 2 hours

First, make the curry powder. Toast all the spices in a dry frying pan until aromatic and golden brown. Move the spices around the pan with a wooden spoon, being careful not to burn them. Place in a grinder or food processor and grind to a fine powder, then set aside.

Place the sweet potato in a separate saucepan and cover with water. Bring to the boil over a high heat, then reduce to a simmer for 5 minutes. The sweet potato should be slightly cooked but still firm, it will cook further when added to the curry later. Drain and set aside.

Place a large saucepan or wok over medium heat and add the coconut oil or ghee. Once hot, add the onion and garlic and cook until brown. Turn down the heat to low and add the Sri Lankan curry powder, turmeric and chilli and cook for about 10 minutes, gently stirring with your trusty wooden spoon to prevent the mix from sticking. Add the coconut milk and allow to simmer for 5 minutes. Now add the ginger, cinnamon, curry leaves, lime juice and fish sauce. Continue to simmer, then add the sweet potato and simmer away for a further 10 minutes.

Remove the fish from the fridge and pat dry with paper towel. Add it to the simmering saucy pot of loveliness you have just created. Simmer and cook for around 10 minutes, or until the fish is just cooked through. Be careful not to overcook! Season with salt and pepper to taste.

Serve with quinoa or brown rice, or a combination of both, or on its own, and garnish with sliced green chilli (such as jalapeno or serrano pepper). Look to the heavens and thank Chimpdad and all of Sri Lanka for this bowl of greatness.

You can make a big jar of Sri Lankan curry powder in advance to use as a seasoning for other dishes; it stores for months in an airtight jar in the pantry. Cauliflower florets cooked in a saucepan with a teaspoon of the curry powder and some coconut oil is delicious.

HAZELNUTS

What rich little honey-coloured kernels! Hazelnuts are a perfect, filling snack eaten raw with a little fruit and are also just as nice lightly toasted and tossed through a salad.

Nutritionally, hazelnuts are wonderful, containing protein, healthy fat, fibre and carbohydrate to keep you filled and fueled. They're also rich in micronutrients, including B-group vitamins (particularly B9), antioxidant vitamin E (including the fat to absorb this fat-soluble nutrient) and a wealth of minerals including manganese, potassium, calcium, copper, iron, magnesium and zinc. Hazelnuts contain the flavonoid quercertin, an incredibly versatile compound widely used in the management of heart conditions, which helps manage and balance cholesterol levels, diabetes, eye conditions, mental health conditions, asthma and other respiratory issues, viral infections … the list is endless.

TORTA GIANDUIA

3 cups hazelnut meal

¼ cup cacao powder, plus extra for dusting

¼ teaspoon sea salt

8 teaspoons gluten-free baking powder

4 eggs

½ cup maple syrup

4–8 teaspoons vanilla paste

¼ cup coconut oil, melted and cooled

extra hazelnuts and raspberries, if desired, for serving

Gianduia is the Italian name for the amalgamation of chocolate and hazelnut. Yes, they have a word for this glorious marriage of two flavours. This in anyone's language is Nutella. So torta gianduia is a Nutella cake. Have you ever heard of anything so tempting in your life? This marvel of human creation is gluten-free, grain-free and dairy-free.

Preheat the oven to 170°C (340°F). In a large bowl, mix together the dry ingredients — hazelnut meal, cacao powder, salt, baking powder — with a wooden spoon until well combined. In a separate bowl, whisk together the eggs, maple syrup and vanilla paste. Add the melted but not hot (or else you will cook the eggs) coconut oil.

Fold the wet ingredients slowly into the dry, and mix for a couple of minutes to ensure there are no 'dry' spots and is well-combined.

Pour the batter into a cake tin lined with baking paper and bake for 45 to 50 minutes. The lower the heat and the longer the cooking time the better, to ensure the cake is baked all the way through. Test whether it is cooked by inserting a skewer or sharp knife into the centre of the cake; if it comes out clean, it's ready to roll.

Remove the cake from the oven and allow to sit in the tin for 5 minutes, then turn out onto a serving plate or wire rack. Resist the urge to eat the entire cake right now, and fend off loved ones who have similar intentions. Ice (frost) it if you like (a suitable icing/frosting would be the whipped coconut used in the Carrot Cake recipe (see p. 44) with 1 tablespoon of cacao mixed in) but this rich cake is delicious simply dusted with a little cacao powder and topped with some fresh raspberries and toasted hazelnuts. This cake is absolutely divine on a rainy afternoon with some warm Turmeric Milk (see p. 183) or Digestive Fennel Tea (see p. 197).

the benefits

reduce cholesterol

❋

diabetes management

❋

skin health

ALMONDS

Almonds are power packs of nature. These powerful little morsels are super nutrient-dense, providing a heap of protein, omega-3 fatty acids, biotin (a B vitamin that aids the metabolism of fats and carbohydrates and gives you the thick, shiny hair of a shampoo commercial), vitamin E (antioxidant, immune-boosting, skin-supercharging, cholesterol-reducing wonder vitamin), manganese (another powerful antioxidant that helps out in the body's production of energy, and important for joints), magnesium (a muscle and nervous system relaxant, this guy will reduce your chances of heart attack and plays a part in hundreds of different enzymatic reactions), molybdenum (another important co-factor in enzyme activity and inflammation reduction) and fibre (reducing cholesterol, helping out with weight management and preventing digestive complaints).

Almonds are a perfect snack for people trying to manage their weight for a number of different reasons: as mentioned they contain biotin, which helps to burn excess energy, and also deliver a nice balance of fats, protein and fibre to keep you full and less likely to binge-eat throughout the day. They lower cholesterol, and reduce your risk of diabetes and heart disease (a major cause of death in the West).

To make your almonds even more nutritionally available, it is a great idea to 'activate' them by soaking them overnight in some filtered water. This begins the germination process, releasing the enzymes that make these magical nuts easier to digest and improves the availability of the nutrients to be easily broken down and used by the body.

Eat almonds raw, on their own or in a trail mix. Make your own almond milk as a dairy substitute, then use the leftover solid pulp to bake the following Gluten-free Bread or as a substitute for plain (all-purpose) flour in cakes and slices. Sprinkle the raw kernels on salads or over steamed or sautéed vegetables to add healthy fats, protein and extra nutrients.

GLUTEN-FREE BREAD

3 cups almond flour

optional: to make multigrain bread add ¾ cup mixture of pepitas, sunflower seeds, poppy seeds, sesame seeds and linseeds/flaxseeds, which can also be sprinkled on top

1 teaspoon gluten-free baking powder

½ teaspoon sea salt

3 eggs, at room temperature

1 teaspoon honey

1 tablespoon unfiltered apple cider vinegar

Preheat the oven to 150°C (300°F). In a large mixing bowl, combine the almond flour, seed mixture (if desired), baking powder and salt. In a separate bowl, whisk together the eggs, honey and cider vinegar until well combined. Next, stir the egg mixture into the almond flour mixture with a wooden spoon, knead gently in the bowl with your hands to form a dough. After a couple of minutes a ball of dough will form using gentle pressure against the side of the bowl. Do not over-knead, but ensure that all ingredients are well combined.

Place the dough into a loaf tin lined with baking paper and bake for approximately 1 hour, depending on the depth of your tin. To test if it is cooked, poke the centre of the loaf with a skewer, which should come out cleanly when the bread is ready.

Serve hot with a lick of organic butter, or a little extra virgin olive oil, sliced ripe tomato, sea salt and basil.

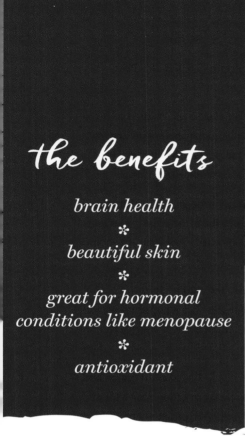

the benefits

brain health

✳

beautiful skin

✳

*great for hormonal
conditions like menopause*

✳

antioxidant

WALNUTS

Walnuts are another of the foods that resemble the organ whose health they contribute towards. These wizened-looking nuts are just perfect for the brain, thanks to their omega-3 fatty acids and vitamin E content, and those same nutrients do wonders for skin health, too.

They are highly antioxidant thanks to their vitamin E and manganese content, with those two key nutrients also making them a beautiful snack for those going through menopause. Vitamin E may help to reduce common menopause symptoms such as hot flushes and itchy skin, while protecting the heart and brain at an age where women need to be more vigilant at protecting these vital organs. Walnuts promote thick, glossy hair thanks to their biotin and omega-3 content; they help ward off heart disease due to their omega-3, potassium and magnesium; and are indicated in the prevention of diabetes, weight management and bone strength with their combination of calcium and magnesium.

Walnuts have a slightly sweet, slightly bitter flavour and crunchy texture that lends itself to salads and smoothies, or as a satisfying snack on their own. When crumbled, they provide a perfect, healthy substitute biscuit base (crust) for cheesecakes and slices (dessert bars).

CHILLI CHOCOLATE PIE

CRUST

1 cup raw walnuts

1 cup macadamia nuts

5 Medjool dates, pitted

1 teaspoon ground cinnamon

pinch of sea salt

½ cup shredded coconut

FILLING

1 x 400 ml (13½ oz) can coconut cream — you will need a total of 1 cup of coconut cream

¼ cup coconut oil

10–12 Medjool dates, pitted

250 g (9 oz) dark chocolate (80–90% cacao content)

2 teaspoons vanilla paste

pinch of cinnamon

1 teaspoon cayenne pepper (or more if you love chilli as much as I do; taste the mixture and adjust to your liking)

NOTE: THIS RECIPE REQUIRES OVERNIGHT REFRIGERATION

Prepare the coconut cream by placing the can in the fridge the night before you wish to make the pie. This will solidify the cream and help you separate the cream from the water; the next morning, simply pour off the coconut water and keep to use in something else.

First, make the crust. In a food processor, process the walnuts and macadamia nuts until fine and crumbly. Add the other crust ingredients and blend until well chopped up and combined. The mixture should clump together when pinched.

Press the crust mixture into the base and along the sides of a springform cake tin. (I have a brilliant one that has a pop-out bottom! Recommended.) Once evenly pressed out, place in the fridge to chill for 30 minutes.

Place a small saucepan over a low heat and add the coconut cream and coconut oil. Heat until just melted, then transfer to a food processor and add the dates, chocolate, vanilla, cinnamon and cayenne pepper. Blend until smooth and creamy. It will look a little thin but the coconut oil will solidify later in the fridge. Pour the filling mixture into your chilled pie crust, and return to the depths of the fridge to chill for at least 2 to 3 hours ... overnight is best.

Enjoy.

the benefits

cardio-protective
*
healthy skin and hair
*
good immune function

BRAZIL NUTS

When I think of brazil nuts, I think skin health, heart health, diabetes and hormone modulation. These beautiful nuts have a wonderful flavour similar to coconut, but with the texture of macadamia nuts, and are incredibly high in that skin-loving antioxidant nutrient selenium, as well as being packed full of healthy mono-unsaturated fats like oleic acid and palmitoleic acid, both of which are cardio-protective, promote healthy skin, hair and immune system, and are anti-inflammatory. These fats are also invaluable for diabetics and those with insulin-related hormonal conditions, as palmitoleic acid in particular has been shown to increase insulin sensitivity.

Brazil nuts contain manganese, magnesium, copper, a range of B-group vitamins, zinc (more skin-loving, immunity-promoting goodness!), potassium, calcium, iron and phosphorous, making them a fabulous snack to ward off hunger pangs and sugar cravings, and increase energy levels, while dosing up on antioxidants and immune-boosting nutrients. Most lovely of all is the earthy, nutty flavor of brazil nuts, which are plain gorgeous when dipped in healthy homemade chocolate (see the recipe on p. 118), chopped and sprinkled into a chia pudding or on top of a fruit salad, or as a yummy addition to a trail mix.

DECADENT BRAZIL NUT TRUFFLES

12 Medjool dates, pitted

12 raw brazil nuts

150 g (5 oz) very dark (80% cacao content) chocolate

coconut oil

shredded coconut, toasted, or chopped brazil nuts

Simple, sweet and satisfying, these truffles are certain to kick the occasional sweet craving to the curb. These wonderful little darlings offer a handy little package of minerals, fibre, protein and good fat. They still contain a fair bit of naturally occurring sugar though, so don't eat them all at once!

MAKES 12 TRUFFLES

Push a brazil nut into the end of each date. Next, place a small saucepan over low heat, add the chocolate and a little coconut oil and gently melt. (You can also make your own chocolate, which will be liquid at first; see note below.)

Place the melted chocolate in a small bowl, and place the shredded coconut in another small bowl. Now dip each date first into the chocolate, using a toothpick or spoon. (I'm a little rougher than that, and will dip a whole date in, let it get totally covered in chocolate then fish it out with a spoon.) Now dip into the coconut (or extra chopped brazil nuts). The coconut can be sprinkled on top instead, if preferred.

Have a tray lined with baking paper ready, and place your dipped dates onto the baking paper. Place your little chocolatey love-logs in the fridge to chill for around 10 minutes, or if this is a dire treat emergency, place in the freezer for around 2 minutes.

Note: you can make your own healthy chocolate by simply melting together equal parts of maple syrup, cacao and coconut oil.

CASHEW NUTS

the benefits

enzymatic function support

*

antioxidant

*

muscle function

Cashew nuts are incredibly versatile — they're lovely as a snack raw, lightly toasted and popped in a stir-fry or any kind of salad, and are especially important in maintaining the sanity of new vegans as they make a fabulous substitute for dairy in vegan cheese. Cashew nuts are beyond decadent when whipped into a butter (celery boats, anyone?) and when used to make vegan cheesecake. I actually love vegan cheesecake more than, well, *cheese* cheesecakes these days.

Cashew nuts provide handy nutrients like copper (utilized by the body as a co-factor for enzymes, especially in the production of energy — see 'The lowdown' on the opposite page), phosphorous (for healthy bones and teeth), zinc (an incredibly important mineral for reproductive health, immunity, skin health and as a co-factor for important enzymes), magnesium and manganese.

These little kidney-shaped dudes also provide lovely monounsaturated fats for your cardiovascular system and keep you filled and fuelled for longer, reducing the likelihood of a chocolate feeding frenzy.

VEGAN LEMON CHEESECAKE

CRUST

1 cup Medjool dates

½ teaspoon nutmeg

2 cups walnuts (almonds and macadamias work, too, or try a combination of all three)

FILLING

2 cups raw cashew nuts, soaked in water overnight

juice and zest of 1½ lemons

½ cup maple syrup

4 teaspoons vanilla paste

12 teaspoons coconut oil

¼ cup water

extra lemon to garnish, if desired

THIS RECIPE REQUIRES SOAKING OVERNIGHT, PLUS A LONG CHILLING TIME

First, make the crust. In a food processor, blend all crust ingredients until the mixture clumps together when pinched. Press the mixture into the bottom of a springform cake tin and place in the fridge or freezer while you make the filling.

Drain and rinse the cashew nuts then place in the food processor and blend until a buttery paste forms, slowly adding water as needed. Keep blending until the mixture is very smooth and no lumps remain. Now add the lemon juice and zest, maple syrup, vanilla paste and coconut oil and keep blending.

Remove the crust from the fridge or freezer. Pour the filling into the crust, and place in the freezer for at least 3 hours, or ideally overnight.

Take out of the freezer 15 minutes prior to serving, and garnish with very thinly sliced lemon peel or lemon zest.

Vegan Lemon Cheesecake p. 121

the benefits

antioxidant

❋

skin health

❋

immune function

❋

healthy metabolism

MACADAMIA NUTS

Full disclosure: I am thoroughly biased when it comes to macadamia nuts. They are hands down my favourite nut. I get full-blown macadamia nut cravings like you wouldn't believe. I adore everything about these milky-coloured little orbs: their texture, and most of all their taste. They are buttery and creamy and go with everything.

Macadamia nuts are the only large-scale commercially grown Australian native food, and they're now grown all over the world. These beautiful nuts contain monounsaturated fats for cardiovascular health and lowering cholesterol, including the monounsaturated fatty acid palmitoleic acid. Palmitoleic acid increases the body's metabolism of fat, which is helpful if you are trying to manage weight. Macadamia nuts also contain antioxidant flavonoids, vitamin A precursors, iron, protein, some B vitamins, selenium (for cognitive function, immunity, a healthy reproductive system and glowing skin), absorbable calcium, phosphorous, magnesium and potassium.

There are myriad ways to enjoy macadamia nuts: raw on their own as a snack (try to stop at a handful if you can ... don't ever try chocolate-coated macadamia nuts because you might not ever stop!); raw and chopped in a salad; or thrown into a tray of roasting vegetables 10 minutes before they are done.

BAKED APPLES WITH
MACADAMIA NUT CRUMBLE

5–6 dates, pitted and chopped

¾ cup raw macadamias

1 teaspoon cinnamon

⅛–¼ cup coconut oil

4 medium-sized Granny Smith apples (or any good cooking apple)

1 tablespoon shredded coconut

optional: extra pinch of nutmeg and/or allspice

SERVES 4

Preheat the oven to 170°C (340°F). First, make the crumble. In a bowl, mix together the dates, macadamia nuts, coconut oil, cinnamon and optional spices (if desired), then set aside.

Prepare your apples by gently scoring the skin horizontally around the apple (around its equator, if you will). Very carefully cut out the core of the apple with a paring knife. I'm going to say very carefully again, because it's important to take care while performing this task if you like all of your fingers to stay attached to your body.

Stand the apples in a casserole dish or baking tray and fill them with the crumble mix, using a teaspoon or your fingers. Cover with a lid or foil and bake for 30 minutes or until your apples are a melty, soft ball of dessert deliciousness.

Serve on their own or with a dollop of organic pastured pouring cream or natural full-fat yoghurt.

the benefits

heart health

✳

skin health

✳

eye health

✳

bone health

✳

energy production

PISTACHIO NUTS

These gorgeous jewels of the nut world, so prominent in Middle Eastern cuisine, have a rich flavour different from other nuts and provide a spectacular, fresh pea-green colour feature to anything they are added to. Pistachio nuts are a perfect snack for anyone at risk of diabetes, hypertension, metabolic syndrome or heart disease, thanks to their good balance of macronutrients (protein, fibre, fat and carbohydrate) to balance blood sugar, their LDL cholesterol-lowering abilities, and their healthy monounsaturated fats like oleic acid, which is great for maintaining a healthy coronary system. They provide an abundance of micronutrients, too, like potassium, phosphorous, vitamin A precursors and carotenoids like lutein and zeaxanthin for extraordinary eye health, along with B-group vitamins, calcium, iron, zinc, vitamin C, Vitamin E, magnesium, copper, manganese, vitamin K and selenium. They're antioxidant and, with that enormous range of nutrients, are helpful for a huge array of health concerns from skin and eye conditions and weight management, and help to support healthy digestion, good immune function and energy production.

These brilliant, unsung heroes deserve a lot more attention than they currently get amongst their nutty companions. Pistachio nuts are fantastic used in salads, sprinkled on top of steamed vegetables, crushed and used as a crumb for coating lamb and make the greatest gelato flavour in existence.

RAW TURKISH DELIGHT

1 cup coconut oil, softened or melted

approximately ½ cup cacao powder

approximately ⅓ cup maple syrup (honey won't work in this instance as it crystalizes when chilled)

big pinch each of cinnamon, nutmeg and sea salt, if desired

2–3 tablespoons shredded coconut

½ cup whole shelled pistachio nuts

⅓ cup dried cranberries, goji berries or cherries (fresh or dried) or a mix of all three

dried rose petals to serve (not essential, just very pretty)

MAKES 8–10 SERVES
NOTE: THIS RECIPE REQUIRES CHILLING TIME.

In a bowl, mix together the coconut oil, cacao powder and maple syrup until very well combined, tasting as you go. If the mixture is too bitter, add a little extra coconut oil and maple syrup; if too sweet, add a little more coconut oil, cacao and salt, and so forth. Add the spices and shredded coconut and mix until well combined.

Place a sheet of baking paper over a dinner plate or tray (it will need to fit in your fridge or freezer), and pour the chocolate mixture over the baking paper. Once settled, press the pistachios, berries and/or cherries into the chocolate mixture and sprinkle the rose petals on to the top. Freeze or refrigerate until the chocolate mixture is completely solid (for at least 20 minutes in the fridge or 5 minutes in the freezer).

Serve in chunks whenever chocolate craving hits. Gently break off pieces with your hands, or use a sharp knife that's been run under hot water for a minute or so.

CHIA SEEDS

Chia seeds have changed my life. These incredible little seeds mean that I can eat dessert for breakfast in the form of chia puddings, and be all the healthier for it. Glory. hallelujah! A chocolate pudding flavoured with cacao one day, vanilla bean and manuka honey the next; life is much, much better since I got on board the chia train.

These South American friends dish up some fabulous nutrients, including plenty of fibre and protein to keep you feeling full until lunchtime, some good absorbable calcium, magnesium to calm us down, phosphorous and manganese — which makes for some delicious antioxidant power! The magical absorption power of the chia seed is what makes for its beautiful pudding texture; these babies can absorb up to 27 times their weight in water, so 2 tablespoons of dry chia seeds is more than enough for a delicious, filling breakfast when soaked in some coconut milk and mixed with other delicious natural flavours like berries and cinnamon.

Chia seeds are very high in omega-3 fatty acids, although in chia seeds it is in the form of alpha-linoleic acid, or ALA, which does not convert very readily to the most therapeutic form of omega-3 (see 'The lowdown' on the opposite page), but there are still some measurable benefits from ALA like better respiratory function and a reduction in the risk of heart disease by helping to reduce high blood pressure and atherosclerosis.

Chia seeds make a wonderful substitute for eggs as a binding agent in foods for vegans or the egg intolerant amongst us — generally the replacement ratio is 4 teaspoons of chia seeds per egg being replaced.

It's important to pay attention to how you're consuming your chia (and flaxseeds/linseeds for that matter). Chia (and most nuts/seeds) are bound by a layer of natural chemical substance called phytate, which binds to minerals that are consumed, making them less absorbable to the body. The phytate has to be broken down before consumption otherwise you're not going to get all the nutrients that are contained in the seed or nut — they will simply pass through the digestive system without being absorbed. So either grind them up in a coffee grinder or food processor, or with a mortar and pestle, before adding to your green smoothie or breakfast. Chia puddings that are soaked overnight are fine.

THE LOWDOWN: OMEGA-3 FATTY ACIDS

It is important to note that there are different forms of omega-3 fatty acids. The types of omega-3 in cold water fish are EPA (eicosapentaenoic acid — the 'heart health' omega) and DHA (docosahexaenoic acid —the brain, eyes and skin health omega). The plant source of omega-3 is ALA (a-linolenic acid). ALA can convert to EPA and DHA in the human body, but you must consume a significant amount of ALA, you must be in good health (conversion doesn't happen as readily if your body is taking nutrients to repair damage elsewhere in the body) and you must eat all of the required co-factors for conversion to take place. Even after all that, the conversion rate of ALA to DHA is around 1 per cent, and to EPA around 5 per cent.

There are fewer studies relating to the health benefits of ALA than there are on DHA/EPA. However, the evidence from the most recent studies relating to ALA have suggested it has a marked effect on reducing the risk of cardiovascular disease.

GINGER AND PEAR
CHIA PUDDINGS

⅓ cup white chia seeds

2½ cups coconut milk (or 1½ cups coconut milk and 1 cup filtered water)

4 dates, pitted

1 teaspoon vanilla paste

2 tablespoons honey or maple syrup

2 pears, grated

1 knob of ginger, peeled and finely grated.

These protein-packed puddings are wonderful for breakfast or as a dessert.

SERVES 6

NOTE: THIS RECIPE REQUIRES OVERNIGHT SOAKING. PREPARE AHEAD OF TIME AND HAVE IN THE FRIDGE FOR BREAKFASTS ON THE GO.

In a large bowl (the chia seeds will expand) place the chia seeds, coconut milk, dates, vanilla and honey or maple syrup. Stir until thoroughly mixed and all chia seeds are 'wet'. Refrigerate overnight.

The next day, stir through the grated pear and ginger. Divide the mixture into individual jars or serving glasses as is or, for a better consistency (and better absorption of nutrients from the chia seeds), place the entire mixture in a food processor and blend until smooth.

Top each serving with a tablespoon of coconut milk and a sprinkling of nutmeg or powdered ginger if desired.

the benefits

brain function

✳

heart health

✳

skin health

✳

immunity

FLAXSEEDS/ LINSEEDS

Flaxseeds (or linseeds; they're the same thing) are tiny brown antioxidant powerhouses, adding lovely texture and fibre to everything they are added to. They are high in omega-3 fatty acids, which reduce cognitive decline, protect the heart, regulate cholesterol and aid a range of health issues including autoimmune disease, neurological disorder, behavioural disorders, anxiety and depression. Flaxseeds also offer a bunch of fibre, aiding weight loss, cholesterol balance and digestive function, and also contain manganese, magnesium and selenium.

As with chia seeds, these lovely little seeds can sometimes be used in recipes calling for eggs as the binding ingredient; a godsend for vegans and those with egg allergies. In order to best absorb the nutrients of flaxseeds, be sure to thoroughly soak or finely grind the seeds. Try not to buy the pre-ground flax meal, as the oils in flaxseeds begin to oxidize once exposed to air and light, and will go rancid (I personally don't want to be eating anything with the word rancid attached to it). Freshly grind at home!

Be aware that flaxseeds are high in phytoestrogens that can affect those who are estrogen dominant. This can be great for healthy women going through menopause, but not so great for a woman with Polycystic Ovarian Syndrome. Eat sparingly or consult a professional if you are unsure.

FLAX CRACKERS

2 cups flaxseeds/linseeds

½ teaspoon sea salt

1 teaspoon garlic powder

seasonings: poppy seeds, dried rosemary, chilli (chili pepper), cumin seeds, etc.

4 teaspoons extra virgin olive oil

1 cup filtered water

MAKES ABOUT 30 CRACKERS

Preheat the oven to 180°C (350°F). Grind the flaxseeds in a food processor until they form a fine-as-you-can-get powder. Place the flaxseed powder into a large bowl with the remaining dry ingredients and mix to combine. Make a well in the centre, then slowly add the oil and water incrementally while mixing, until a nice dough forms.

Line a baking tray with baking paper, then using a knife or spatula spread your cracker mix on the tray as thinly as possible. At this stage, you can score the crackers into squares or rectangles so they can be snapped into uniform shapes, or if you're feeling rustic just break off great hunks of cracker from your giant mother-cracker once it emerges from the oven.

Bake in the oven for around 15 minutes, depending on how thinly the mixture is spread on the tray. Remove from the oven and allow to cool for a few minutes.

PEPITAS

Little green pepitas are the seeds from pumpkin (winter squash) and are packed to their little green eyeballs in minerals (in particular) and vitamins.

If you are of the vegan or vegetarian persuasion, then I dearly hope these little darlings are on a regular rotation in your diet as they are a great source of zinc. Zinc is vitally important for countless different functions of the body, including as a co-factor for the production of lots of different hormones. Zinc is really important for skin health and a healthy immune system, and is also vitally important for fertility in both men and women, but especially for young, sexually active men.

Pepitas have been found to be antibacterial, antifungal and antiviral, giving another level of immune support. Pepitas also offer a good amount of manganese, magnesium, iron, potassium and vitamin E, so are wonderfully antioxidant, besides adding a little colour and crunch to salads, trail mix and whatever else you want to add them to.

the benefits

reproductive health

❋

beautiful skin

❋

improve immune function

CHILLI MAPLE PEPITAS

1 cup pepitas (pumpkin seeds)

1 tablespoon coconut oil, melted

1 teaspoon maple syrup

1 teaspoon smoked paprika

1 teaspoon cayenne pepper

This is a lovely, crunchy little snack on its own, or add it to a Mexican salsa, on top of a salad or as a textural addition to soup.

MAKES APPROXIMATELY 1 CUP

Preheat the oven to 170°C (340°F). Line a baking tray with baking paper and spread the pepitas on the tray. Place in the oven and roast for about 8 minutes.

Remove from the oven and place in a bowl while leaving the oven on. Add all the other ingredients and mix thoroughly with a spoon (not your hands ... its hot!). Again, line the baking tray with baking paper and spread the pepitas evenly on the tray. Return to the oven and roast for another 8 to 10 minutes. The total roasting time shouldn't exceed 20 minutes.

SESAME SEEDS

Adorable little sesame seeds are never far from my grasp in the kitchen; I keep a huge jar of them handy and sprinkle them on everything from salads, breakfasts, cakes, condiments and cooked vegetables (they add a heavenly crunch to the Garlicky Greens on p. 195). Their flavour and texture is a wonderful accompaniment. They are also teeny tiny mineral powerhouses.

the benefits

bone health

✳

energy production

✳

skin health

Sesame seeds are just brilliant at maintaining healthy bones (especially when combined with greens) and staving off osteoporosis thanks to their generous amount of absorbable calcium. They also contain high levels of copper (so be aware of this if you are deficient in zinc, as this can out throw the zinc–copper ratio), which assists in energy production and plays an important role in assisting anti-inflammatory processes in the body. Sesame seeds also provide magnesium, phosphorous, iron, selenium and fibre, as well as some helpful phytosterols to help lower cholesterol. They are so easy to incorporate into the daily diet and I rely on them so much, purely for their culinary enhancement properties (the beautiful, slightly oily, crunchy *pop*!), that it warrants a full-blown kitchen meltdown if I run out.

Sesame seeds form the basis of tahini, which you can make at home if you have a powerful blender. Keep a jar of black and regular sesame seeds at home and get sprinkling!

DUKKAH

½ cup hazelnuts, chopped

⅓ cup sesame seeds

2 tablespoons cumin seeds

2 tablespoons coriander seeds

1 teaspoon smoked paprika

1–2 teaspoons pepper

1 teaspoon sea salt flakes

Dukkah is a flavour-packed Middle Eastern spice mixture used to add crunch and taste to various foods to make them far and away more interesting. Traditionally used as a dip for bread (the bread is dipped into olive oil, then into a pot of dukkah), you can use dukkah as a rub on all kinds of meat and fish, as a salad topper, or on top of Spanish Baked Eggs (see p. 80).

MAKES APPROXIMATELY 1 CUP

Place the hazelnuts and sesame seeds in a frying pan over a medium heat, stirring with a wooden spoon for about 3 minutes. Next add the cumin seeds and coriander seeds and toast gently for another 3 minutes. Be careful not to burn!

Remove the ingredients to a mortar and pestle and add the paprika, pepper and salt. Grind, and you have yourself a jar full of the finest dukkah in the land.

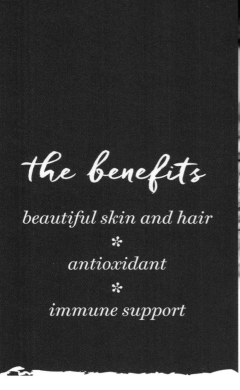
SUNFLOWER SEEDS

How wonderful that nature makes something as breathtakingly beautiful as the sunflower, then leaves us with something as yum and nutritious as the sunflower seed. The seeds of this incredible and enormous flower are loaded with essential nutrients, especially the highly antioxidant vitamin E, which is important for a good immune system, reduces the risk of heart disease and stroke, is wonderful for healthy skin, hair and epithelial linings, and can be really effective for the management of premenstrual syndrome and menopausal symptoms. As a fat-soluble vitamin, vitamin E needs a bit of fat to be absorbed by the body; sunflower seeds have that covered by packaging vitamin E with some healthy fat so it can be utilized by your body.

Brilliant little sunflower seeds also provide copper, B vitamins, manganese, selenium, phosphorous, and magnesium.

Sunflower seeds are wonderful as a topper for a chia seed pudding breakfast, are lovely raw on their own as a snack, and provide a gorgeous nutty flavour to breakfasts, lunches (sprinkled in a salad) or as a crunchy crust on fish or lamb.

SUNFLOWER SEED CRUSTED LAMB

1 tablespoon almond meal

1 sprig rosemary,
finely chopped

1 cup sunflower seeds,
roughly chopped

sea salt and pepper, to taste

1 egg

8 lamb chops, frenched
(ask your butcher to do
this)

extra virgin olive oil, to fry

leafy green salad, to serve

SERVES 4

In a bowl or on a plate, combine the almond meal, rosemary, sunflower seeds, salt and pepper. Crack the egg into a bowl (large enough to fit one lamb chop at a time) and beat well with a fork. Coat each little lamb chop first in the beaten egg, then in the seed crust mixture. Don't be shy now: ensure the chop is well coated.

Place a frying pan over medium heat, then add a little olive oil. Add the lamb chops and cook until browned, turning to cook the other side. (Lamb should be served slightly pink inside. In my humble opinion, there are few abominations in this world worse than overcooked meat.)

Serve these simple, delicious morsels on a big bed of leafy green salad.

POPPY SEEDS

Although they are small in size, poppy seeds are big in
nutrients and have a unique, nutty flavour, crunchy texture,
and add a certain something sprinkled over any kind of
salad. I keep a jar handy for just this purpose and not once
have I regretted it.

These adorable little seeds contain a bunch of essential
nutrients, including the all-important omega-3 fatty acids
that are vital for a range of health concerns including depression, heart conditions, stroke,
all kinds of inflammation, joint and skin conditions, and form part of the membrane
of every cell in the body. If you need another reason to eat these helpful little men, they
also contain phosphorous and absorbable calcium for a healthy skeleton and teeth; fibre,
important for digestion, cholesterol regulation, detoxification and weight management;
iron, responsible for carrying oxygen all over the body via our blood; and oleic acid, a
monounsaturated fatty acid that avocados and olive oil also contain, which is indicated in
the management of diabetes and heart conditions.

I also love their black-grey colour, which provides the most wonderful contrast next to
bright green vegetables, as in the incredible and versatile Crunchy Poppy Seed Gremolata
on the opposite page.

CRUNCHY POPPY SEED GREMOLATA

small bunch of broccolini, stalks only (use the tops raw in a salad or other recipe)

¼ cup poppy seeds

¼ cup sesame seeds

¼ cup pepitas (pumpkin seeds)

1 large lemon

sea salt and pepper, to taste (plus chilli flakes, if desired)

2–3 teaspoons unfiltered apple cider vinegar or white wine vinegar

2 tablespoons extra virgin olive oil

MAKES 1 LARGE JAR; KEEPS IN THE FRIDGE FOR UP TO 1 WEEK

Bring a saucepan of water to the boil then add the broccolini stalks and lightly blanch. You want them to be bright green and crunchy but ever so slightly cooked. Drain and allow to cool completely, then cut into very thin rounds so they look like very small green coins.

Mix together the poppy seeds, sesame seeds and pepitas in a bowl, then finely grate in the zest of the lemon. Juice the lemon and add the juice to the bowl. Add seasoning, then the vinegar and oil, and mix thoroughly with a spoon.

Enjoy as a topping on lots of different meals, including on top of baked chicken or fish, on different kinds of salad (including Home-cured Beetroot Salad on p. 49), sprinkle on top of pumpkin soup to add interest, or use as you would dukkah.

7. Fruits

Fruits are quite simply nature's candy. Sweet, colourful, refreshing and full of vital nutrients that support so many important functions of the body and prevent disease, while helpfully flushing us with skin-loving nutrients to boot. Fruity goodness will keep us feelin' good, lookin' good. They're so versatile, can be enjoyed cooked or fresh and are perfect to keep your body properly fuelled and energized during or after intense exercise.

the benefits

antioxidant
✽
skin health
✽
cancer protective
✽
anti-inflammatory
✽
cardio-protective
✽
great for diabetics

BLUEBERRIES

Blueberries are always somewhere on the list of the latest 'superfoods' and for very good reason: these plump, purplish little berries are not only packed with vitamin C, manganese, fibre and vitamin K, they contain incredibly high levels of over fifteen different types of antioxidant phytonutrients, such as quercetin (anti-inflammatory, pain relief, cardio-protective, reduces blood pressure, increases immunity and eases respiratory conditions), resveratrol (cardio-protective by strengthening the arteries, as well as being a powerful anti-inflammatory), caffeic acid (immunoregulatory, so fantastic for those with autoimmune conditions as it calms an out-of-control immune response and boosts a sluggish one), cyanidin (a skin-protective chemical which is also great for diabetics and weight management, is anti-inflammatory, immune-boosting and makes our skin beautiful) and kaempferol (especially heart-protective).

Blueberries are gorgeous either fresh or frozen, with frozen blueberries having been shown to possess the same health benefits as fresh. The most important thing when eating blueberries (or any berry, for that matter) is to choose organic — in general, berries are more susceptible to insect attack, so non-organic berries contain a lot of pesticides.

BLUEBERRY PANCAKES

2 eggs

1 ripe banana, mashed with a fork

pinch of cinnamon

1 big handful of blueberries (frozen is fine), plus extra to serve

coconut oil, for frying

optional: 1 tablespoon of maple syrup (not completely necessary; but kids, for example, might like a sweeter version)

Perfect, high protein pancake goodness — just wonderful for your body post-workout.

MAKES APPROXIMATELY
2–3 SMALL PANCAKES

In a bowl, whisk the eggs well. Add the banana and cinnamon (and maple syrup, if desired), and use a hand mixer to blend the mixture until it forms a very smooth paste. If you think you have blended it enough, then blend it some more; if the banana isn't properly integrated, you can end up within distinguishable lumps in your pancakes. Add the blueberries. Don't stir too much or else your pancakes will be blue.

Place a small frying pan over a high heat and add a little coconut oil. Now add a big ladle full of mixture to the pan and allow it to cook. Once bubbles appear on the surface and your pancake looks mostly firm, flip it over with a spatula.

Serve in a stack, with extra blueberries on top and maple syrup if desired.

the benefits

reduce cholesterol

✽

heart health

✽

energy production

✽

digestive health

FIGS

Figs are one of my favourite parts of summer. Fresh, juicy, plump, honey-scented figs straight off the tree are a highly anticipated and appreciated treat from nature. I eat them until my mouth goes numb (not recommended). They're so insanely beautiful to look at too: deep purple on the outside and light green and crimson on the inside.

Before I get too explicit on how much I adore figs, I ought to mention that there are many ways to eat them, both sweet and savoury (if they make it from the tree to our kitchen before I nibble on them): figs, ricotta cheese and honey; figs on a cheese board; fig and goat's cheese gelato; figs with quinoa porridge; figs in a fruit salad situation.

And these genuine beauties pack a nutrient punch, too! Packed full of fibre, figs are great for constipation, high cholesterol and weight management. They also contain some B vitamins to up your energy production, along with copper, manganese and potassium, as if you needed any other reasons to eat them beyond their wonderful taste.

FIG, THYME
AND GOAT'S CHEESE TART

CRUST

½ cup coconut oil, melted

2 eggs

¼ teaspoon sea salt

¾ cup coconut flour, plus a little extra for rolling out

FILLING

small bunch of thyme

extra virgin olive oil

½ leek, green part only, trimmed and chopped into fine half-rounds

4 large or 5 small eggs

¾ cup organic pastured pouring cream

sea salt and pepper, to taste

200 g (7 oz) goat's cheese

4–6 ripe figs, halved

Oh, lordy lord. This visual and edible feast is gluten and grain free.

Preheat the oven to 180°C (350°F). In a bowl, whisk together the coconut oil, eggs, and salt. Slowly but surely, add the coconut flour, mixing the whole time until a ball of dough forms. Turn the dough out onto a clean benchtop or board dusted lightly with extra coconut flour then roll it out slightly, and press it into a pie dish. Place the crust in the oven and bake for 5 to 10 minutes or until perfectly golden brown and crumbly. Keep checking during this time in case an air bubble forms, in my experience a rare but plausible pie affliction — if one develops, just pop it with something sharp. Remove from the oven and set aside to cool, leaving the oven on.

Now make the filling. Remove the leaves from half the bunch of thyme, chop them and set aside. Place a frying pan on a high heat and add a little olive oil. Then add the leek, sautéing until soft. Remove from the frying pan and set aside. In a large bowl, whisk the eggs until well beaten, then slowly add the cream, whisking all the while. Add the leeks, salt and pepper, and finally the thyme leaves.

Pour the egg mixture into the cooled pie crust, then spoon or crumble the goat's cheese evenly over the top. Next, arrange the figs on top of the goat's cheese. Put on your artist's cap and artfully place a few sprigs of thyme on top of the whole marvellous thing. Bake in the oven for 30 minutes or until cooked through — the filling should be firm and not jiggly when cooked. You can place it under a hot grill (broiler) for a minute or two to make the egg filling puff up, but this isn't entirely necessary.

Serve to your most fancy house guests.

KIWI FRUIT

Kiwi fruit are our furry, fuzzy green and yellow berry pals (yes, kiwis are a berry) that add serious credentials to fruit salads and do wondrous things within our body, too.

These hairy little friends are jam-packed with vitamin C (even more so than oranges), vitamin K, copper, fibre, vitamin E, potassium, manganese and folate (B9). Kiwi fruit have plenty of cell-protective antioxidants, and all that fibre is going to provide a food source to beneficial bacteria within the digestive tract, cleaning the bowel as it goes and helping you to feel fuller.

Green kiwi fruit also rather wonderfully contain an enzyme called actinidain, which helps to break down protein once ingested (see 'The lowdown' on p. 154). This enzyme is what makes kiwi fruit a famous meat tenderizer; you can cover any kind of meat in slices of kiwi fruit and in a couple of hours you will have the most tender meat you've ever eaten in your life.

Kiwi fruit are a fabulous addition to a green smoothie, can be eaten on their own or as an all important element to any self-respecting fruit salad.

KIWI QUINOA PORRIDGE

1 cup uncooked quinoa

½ Granny Smith apple, grated

1 teaspoon cinnamon, plus extra to serve (optional: add a pinch of nutmeg if it's handy)

¼ cup shredded coconut

1 tablespoon honey

¼ cup sunflower seeds

3 kiwi fruit, peeled

coconut milk, coconut kefir or full-fat natural yoghurt, to serve

A tongue twister and also a delicious breakfast that will keep you full until at least lunchtime.

SERVES 2 (OR DOUBLE THE INGREDIENT AMOUNTS AND KEEP IN THE FRIDGE; KEEPS FOR UP TO THREE DAYS)

Cook the quinoa in a saucepan with water according to packet instructions. When almost cooked (when most of the water has been absorbed and the quinoa seeds are showing their little white tails), add the grated apple, cinnamon, shredded coconut, honey, sunflower seeds and two of the chopped kiwi fruit. Stir the porridge well.

Once cooked through and the apple and kiwi have softened, place into a bowl and top with coconut milk if desired, plus a slice of the remaining kiwi fruit. I don't cook them all as I want to retain all of their wonderful vitamin C, some of which is destroyed during the cooking process.

PAPAYA

Papaya is one of those 'love it or hate it' foods — I adore papaya, and always have, whereas I have heard others describe them as tasting like feet. They come in several varieties, their flesh ranging in colour from bright yellow to sunset orange, to vibrant grapefruit pink and ruby red.

These sweet-fleshed darlings contain lots of vitamin C, B vitamins (folate, or B9, in particular), beta-carotene, magnesium, potassium and fibre. They also uniquely contain the powerful digestive enzyme called papain (see 'The lowdown' on p. 121). These wonders of the fruit world are particularly helpful for those who have trouble digesting protein on their own (a condition known as protein malabsorption). Papain is more concentrated in ripe fruit rather than younger green papaya, and is even found in the skin and seeds. (Most normal people remove the skin. Not me; I eat every last bit!) The seeds can be eaten, too, and add a slightly bitter, peppery taste, and a crunchy texture, to salads. I have very successfully propagated papaya plants from seeds scooped out of a fruit bought from the market — to try this yourself, just plant the seeds in some seedling potting mix, cover with about 1 cm (½ in.) of potting mix, and see what happens after a couple of weeks!

PRAWN (SHRIMP) AND PAPAYA SALAD

SERVES 2

SALAD

1 tablespoon coconut oil

300 g (10½ oz) prawns (shrimp), deveined and shells removed

optional: chilli flakes

1 small–medium papaya (red or yellow), skin and seeds removed, cut in half lengthways, then horizontally into c-shaped slices

handful of raw almonds or cashews

150 g (5 oz) baby rocket (arugula) leaves

½ red onion, thinly sliced

½ red capsicum (pepper), sliced

1 Lebanese (short) cucumber, sliced into thin diagonal slices

1 avocado, sliced

½ cup basil and/or coriander (cilantro), chopped

DRESSING

juice of 1 lime

2 tablespoons honey

2 tablespoons fish sauce

2 tablespoons sesame oil

1 garlic clove, peeled and finely chopped

1 red chilli (chili pepper), finely chopped

sea salt and pepper, to taste

Make the dressing by whisking together all ingredients (or placing in a screw-top jar and shaking vigorously). Set aside to allow the flavours to combine.

Place a frying pan over high heat and add the coconut oil. Add the prawns and chilli flakes (if desired), and cook for about 5 minutes. Be very careful not to overcook. Once the prawns are just opaque, remove from heat.

In a large bowl combine all other salad ingredients and gently mix. Divide the salad among the serving plates and top with the freshly cooked prawns. Liberally dress each salad and serve immediately.

POMEGRANATE

Behold these incredible rubies of the plant world. Not only do pomegranate seeds make anything they are sprinkled over look gorgeous and tempting, they taste like sweets, are slightly crunchy with a 'pop' in your mouth (in a good way) and they are blow-your-mind good for you.

Pomegranates are seriously antioxidant, containing various polyphenols and flavonoids, and have been studied for their effectiveness in reducing cell growth as well as encouraging cancerous cell death (apoptosis). They protect the heart by lowering high blood pressure, reducing plaque build-up in the arteries and reducing the hardening of arteries. They are also great in the diet of anyone suffering from arthritis or gout, as they are powerfully anti-inflammatory and contain compounds which reduce the production of the enzymes responsible for the degradation of cartilage.

Pomegranates also provide lots of vitamin C, vitamin K, B-group vitamins, vitamin E, potassium, phosphorus and manganese, and are considered one of the great 'beauty foods' thanks to their vitamin C, vitamin E and various antioxidants.

These magical little wonders are fabulous scattered through a variety of salads and in lots of different kinds of desserts and breakfasts, or thrown into a green smoothie to add nutrients and sweetness.

TURKISH SALAD

1½ cups uncooked quinoa

150 g (5 oz) uncooked wild rice

200 g (7 oz) canned chickpeas (garbanzo beans), drained and rinsed

200 g (7 oz) canned lentils, drained and rinsed

½ cup shelled pistachio nuts

4 spring onions (scallions), finely chopped

seeds of 1 pomegranate

100 g (3½ oz) Persian feta cheese, crumbled

½ cup mint leaves, loosely packed, roughly chopped

¾ cup loosely packed flat-leaf parsley, roughly chopped

DRESSING

½ cup extra virgin olive oil

3 tablespoons Dijon mustard

juice of ½ a lemon

sea salt and pepper, to taste

MAKES AN ENORMOUS, FILLING SALAD FOR APPROXIMATELY 5 TO 6 PEOPLE

Cook the quinoa and wild rice according to packet instructions (wild rice will take longer than quinoa). Drain and set aside to cool.

In a large bowl, mix together the quinoa, wild rice, chickpeas, lentils, spring onions, pistachio nuts, pomegranate seeds, mint and parsley. Transfer to a serving platter and top with the feta cheese.

To make the dressing, place all dressing ingredients in a screw-top jar, screw on the lid and shake well. Dress the salad and serve.

the benefits

great for diabetics

❋

skin health

❋

immune function

❋

anti-inflammatory

❋

cancer protective

STRAWBERRIES

Strawberries are small and sweet little antioxidant flavour bombs that taste like summer (and rainbows and happiness). If you cut a strawberry in half it very much resembles a love heart, which is mighty fitting since these little power berries are cardio-protective thanks to their huge antioxidant content and anti-inflammatory attributes.

The antioxidant motherlode in strawberries is thanks to the various and numerous phytonutrients, like anthocyanin (a powerful antioxidant that gives the strawberry its rosy hue while protecting the fruit's cells from damage), resveratrol (the same heart-protecting antioxidant that people call on to justify drinking red wine), caffeic acid (a cancer-hating antioxidant that is also anti-inflammatory and immunomodulatory — great news for those with autoimmune issues), salicylic acid (a pain-relieving, anti-inflammatory antioxidant) as well as flavonols like catechins, kaempferol and quercetin.

Strawberries also contain lots of other good stuff such as abundant vitamin C, manganese (both of which are also antioxidants), fibre, iodine (for a healthy pregnancy and good thyroid function), some B vitamins, potassium, magnesium, phosphorous and omega-3 fatty acids.

These sweet little darlings are great for diabetics and anyone else with insulin-related disorders (such as Polycystic Ovarian Syndrome) as they will help to prevent a big sugar spike. They're perfect to eat on their own, just washed and hulled, or plopped on a chia pudding or into a smoothie.

STRAWBERRY AND SALTED COCONUT SEMIFREDDO

2½ cups coconut cream

200 g (7 oz) organic strawberries, hulled

6 eggs, separated

⅓ cup honey

8 teaspoons vanilla paste

1 teaspoon sea salt, finely ground

⅔ cup coconut flakes (toasted, if preferred)

MAKES APPROXIMATELY 12 SERVES.
NOTE: RECIPE REQUIRES OVERNIGHT FREEZING

Pour the coconut cream into a bowl and place in the freezer for 30 minutes. Meanwhile, prepare the strawberries. Mash half of the strawberries with a fork or in a food processor, and slice or cut into quarters the remaining half, for use as a garnish.

Grease a loaf (bar) tin with butter and line with baking paper, then set aside. In another large mixing bowl, beat the egg yolks, 2 tablespoons of the honey and all the vanilla paste until the mixture becomes foamy and thick.

In a separate mixing bowl (the end result is well worth the washing of all these bowls, I pinky promise), beat the egg whites until peaks form. Add the rest of the honey and beat some more.

After your coconut cream has been chillin' like Bob Dylan for half an hour, remove from the freezer and whisk until it is combined, then add the salt and beat a little more. Now add the egg whites and fold in gently (so as not to lose all of the air that will make your semifreddo light and creamy). Now add the mixture to the bowl with the yolk mixture and gently fold in.

Once uniformly mixed, carefully pour the whole delicious mess into the loaf tin and smooth the top. Place in the freezer and allow to chill for 1 hour, then fold through the mashed strawberries. Return to the freezer and allow to freeze overnight. Turn out onto a pretty serving platter. Top with coconut flakes and remaining strawberries.

GRAPEFRUIT

Grapefruit are not actually related to grapes, but are part of the citrus family, as is obvious to anyone who ever saw one or had a bite of one. The ruby-red fleshed varieties are both prettier to look at than the yellow ones and have a slightly better nutrient profile as they contain antioxidant carotenoids, which give them their gorgeous orangey-pink colour.

Grapefruit is not everyone's favourite fruit, thanks to its slightly bitter taste, but it is well worth including in the diet thanks to its vitamin C, fibre, potassium and some B-group vitamin content, and that bitter taste is going to help stimulate the production of hydrochloric acid and aid digestion.

Antioxidant vitamin C is incredibly important for everything from wound healing, skin cell growth and repair (hello, gorgeous skin), boosting the immune system and reducing inflammation throughout the body. Grapefruit will help reduce cholesterol (thanks to the prebiotic soluble fibre pectin), and famously prevent kidney stones by increasing the excretion of citric acid, which contributes to stone formation.

If you're not a fully fledged member of the grapefruit fan club, a good way to include it in your diet is by throwing a quarter of a grapefruit into a green juice, or in the gorgeous Mediterranean inspired Grapefruit and Fennel Salad on the opposite page.

A word of warning: *Be aware of grapefruit if you take any form of medication (consult your doctor first), as grapefruit can drastically affect the potency of some pharmaceutical drugs, including statins, antidepressants and the birth control pill.*

GRAPEFRUIT AND FENNEL SALAD

2 ruby grapefruit, peeled and membrane removed, sliced into segments

2 fennel bulbs, sliced extra finely, with frilly tops reserved for garnish

2 radishes, sliced extra finely

2–3 tablespoons capers

100 ml (3½ fl oz) extra virgin olive oil

1 tablespoon balsamic vinegar

Feel the freshness! Serve this slightly bitter salad as a light and lovely side to a main of grilled (broiled) fish.

SERVES 4 AS A SIDE SALAD

Ever so gently, arrange the grapefruit segments, fennel, radish slices and capers on a serving platter. Be careful as the grapefruit will fall apart very easily. It doesn't matter too much if you break a couple of segments though, as they will release their gorgeous juice. Dress by splashing over the olive oil and balsamic vinegar.

BANANAS

Bananas are often one of the first solid foods we eat as wee little babies; they're soft, they're sweet and they're loaded with essential nutrients like manganese, vitamin B6, vitamin C, potassium (which they are famous for, but it isn't the banana's most abundant nutrient) and a good amount of fibre. In my observations as a nutritionist, bananas are one of the foods people are least likely to object to; they're a wonderful pre-packaged sweet treat from nature.

Bananas are incredibly versatile. I use them to ripen my avocados, as a ripe banana gives off a hormone which hastens the ripening process for avocados and other fruits too. They can be quickly grabbed while running out the door, and you can bet on any given day I have one stashed in my handbag for hunger emergencies. They're the cornerstone ingredient for any great vegan ice-cream. (Keep some peeled bananas in plastic wrap in the freezer. Blend, and you have a healthy and refreshing icy treat! Add coconut milk, nuts, cacao and/or cacao nibs.). Or simply mash with a fork and mix with some vanilla paste and you have an instant and delicious pudding. They can be sun-dried and taken on hikes and camping trips in place of refined sugar-laden fruit strips, and they're what make the Blueberry Pancakes on page 149 absolutely delicious. And for all these easy ways to add them into your diet, they're wonderful for your body too.

I like to recommend bananas to people who exercise a lot, due to their carbohydrate and sugar content, which is perfect for reloading glycogen stores for your muscles and reducing the incidence of muscle cramps. Thanks to a balance of fibre, the sugar content in bananas is slowly absorbed, reducing the likelihood of high blood sugar. The fibre content in bananas also provides a food source for beneficial bacteria within the digestive tract, and will help you to feel fuller for longer, lessening the chance of going completely off the rails on a sugar bender, if you're prone to them. Plus, the potassium content in bananas makes them wonderful for regulating high blood pressure and preventing atherosclerosis.

PISANG GORENG

1 ripe banana

2 tablespoons coconut oil

optional: shredded coconut, cinnamon, to taste (both highly recommended)

full-fat natural yoghurt, kefir or coconut yoghurt, to serve

I've lost count of how many times I have been to Bali throughout my childhood and adult years. Indonesian cuisine is really comforting food to me. Pisang Goreng translates from Indonesian as fried bananas., and this is one of the many Indonesian foods that I absolutely adore.

Pisang Goreng is best when actually eaten in Indonesia, with those tiny, incredibly sweet Indonesian bananas (the true Indonesian version of Pisang Goreng is deep-fried in a heavy batter, which isn't necessarily a nutritionist's dream!). But when a major sugar craving hits, these little babies can be whipped up very quickly to easily satisfy. I like these after a workout, as the sugar in the banana helps to restock glycogen stores, while the cinnamon helps the body fully utilize those sugars.

SERVES 1

Place a small frying pan over high heat and add the coconut oil. Cut the banana in half lengthways (or in diagonal slices; it's up to you). Place the banana in the frying pan, moving around to prevent burning and to fully coat it in coconut oil. Allow the banana to brown slightly, which means the sugars are caramelizing. When almost cooked, add the cinnamon and shredded coconut.

Enjoy on its own or on top of a small cup of full-fat natural yoghurt, kefir or coconut yoghurt as a breakfast idea.

the benefits

skin health

✳

cancer protective

✳

sleep support

✳

anti-inflammatory

CHERRIES

Beautiful, sweet and shiny, cherries are the basis of one of Neil Diamond's best songs. If I were Neil I would've written a song about cherry baby, too — they have to be one of the most delicious fruits, and they're also vitally good for the body.

Cherries are antioxidant, containing the compounds anthocyanin and quercetin, indicated in the management of an incredible number of disorders and ailments, and are a great inclusion in the diet of anyone wanting to control their weight (they have been studied for their effects against obesity), those who suffer from an inflammatory disorder (especially arthritis and gout) or at risk of heart conditions, as cherries reduce the chances of atherosclerosis (the hardening of the arteries).

Cherries also contain another important antioxidant — melatonin. Melatonin is an incredibly important hormone that the body produces (under the right conditions and with the right balance of nutrients), and it plays a big role in sleep and wake cycles. Melatonin can be a godsend for those who have trouble sleeping, and is also important for those who live near the North and South poles, whose exposure to light varies radically from summer to winter. It is also a great help for those who suffer from jetlag, high blood pressure and anxiety and panic disorders.

Tart or sweet, raw or cooked, cherries are wonderful to eat and contain plenty of vitamin A precursors, vitamin C, vitamin K, vitamin E, B-group vitamins, omega-3 fatty acids, calcium, magnesium, phosphorus and potassium.

GLUTEN, DAIRY AND REFINED SUGAR-FREE CHERRY CAKE

2 cups cherries,
pitted and halved

5 eggs

3 organic oranges
(try to get organic
as the peel is included
in this recipe)

8–12 teaspoons vanilla
paste

⅓ cup honey

2½ cups almond meal

1½ teaspoons gluten-free
baking powder

An easy way to pit your fresh cherries is to place them over the mouth of an empty bottle, with the top of the cherry facing up, then poke the middle with the blunt end of a skewer. The pits should pop out into the bottle.

Place the whole oranges, unpeeled, in a large saucepan of water on the stove. (They will float, but that's okay.) Bring to the boil, then reduce the heat to low and simmer for 1 hour until the oranges are soft. Rescue them from the water with a slotted spoon, place them in a bowl and allow to cool. Once cool (at room temperature) chop into rough chunks, skin and all.

Preheat the oven to 160°C (325°F). In a food processor, blend the oranges until they form a smooth paste, then add the eggs. Blend until the eggs and oranges have formed a loving marriage, then add the vanilla paste and honey. With the food processor running, add the almond flour through the shoot ½ a cup at a time, to ensure it disperses throughout and doesn't form any lumps. Lastly, add your baking powder, then turn off the food processor and gently fold in half of the cherries. (Alternatively, pour the cake mix into the cake tin and plop the cherries on top, pushing some down into the cake. They will sink down further as it cooks.)

Grease a springform cake tin with some butter and line with baking paper. Pour the mixture into the cake tin, place in the oven and allow to bake for 45–50 minutes. The mixture will look very runny; don't be deterred as it firms up in the cooking process. Once the cake is cooked, remove it from the oven and allow it to sit in the tin for at least 1 hour or until the cake has cooled to room temperature. This is an important step, so that your cake does not crack and flop in the middle.

Remove the cake from the tin and carefully place on a serving plate. Garnish with the rest of the cherries, plus other fruits, nuts and edible flowers of your choice. This cake is delicious on its own and really doesn't require icing (frosting), as it is a super-duper moist cake.

PINEAPPLE

If you like piña coladas (I'm sorry, I had to; me and terrible '80s music go together like salt and pepper) then *good* because you will probably also like pineapples, the uniquely shaped tropical fruit that makes me want to swim to the Caribbean right now.

Pineapples are tasty, as sweet as candy, and contain some dandy nutrients, for example an entire day's worth of vitamin C plus extra (these guys overfloweth with vitamin C, and who doesn't need/want/love vitamin C?), manganese, copper, some B vitamins for good measure (those B vitamins and manganese are both essential in the body's production of energy, for all of the fatigued amongst us) as well as some lovely beneficial fibre. But what is outstanding about pineapples is that they are the only naturally occurring source of bromelain, an antioxidant, super anti-inflammatory enzyme that helps the body to break down and utilize protein (it breaks apart the amino acids, allowing our body to combine or carry away each amino acid as it needs). Bromelain is great for soothing muscle injuries and strains, wound healing, osteoarthritis, sinus and respiratory inflammation, asthma, digestive issues and general malabsorption issues. The fabulous combination of bromelain and vitamin C is like a 1-2 punch for most of the aforementioned conditions.

To choose a ripe, sweet pineapple, carefully reach into its spiky crown and clasp one of the inner leaves between your thumb and forefinger. If she gives up her leaf and it pops out easily, you've picked a winner. Once you get it home, do as I do and cut off the leafy top, leaving approximately 1½ to 2 cm (½ –⅔ in.) of the pineapple flesh attached. Pull the bark and flesh away from the bottom of the crown until you reach the white fibrous core. Pop this white part in a jar of water, changing the water occasionally for a couple of weeks or so until your pineapple top has grown roots. Once roots have developed you can pot it in some potting mix or transplant straight into the garden. Pineapples are a gorgeous, hardy and pest-resistant plant that are difficult to kill and in a couple of years you will have an annual crop of pineapples yourself.

the benefits

beautiful skin

✱

anti-inflammatory

✱

immune function

✱

respiratory health

BARBECUED PINEAPPLE WITH CHILLI AND LIME

1 large pineapple

8 skewers, soaked in water for 15 minutes (to avoid burning on the barbecue)

juice of 1 lime

chilli flakes

coconut oil, if required

SERVES 4 AS A SIDE

Trim the top and bark off the pineapple, and cut the flesh into 2 cm (¾ in.) chunks. Thread onto the skewers to make some handy little pineapple kebabs.

Prep your barbecue with a little oil, if it needs it, then heat the barbecue to a high heat and pop on your pineapple skewers. Cook, turning when necessary. Finish by drizzling over lime juice and sprinkling on chilli flakes. Perfectly simple, perfectly yum.

the benefits

antioxidant

✳

immune support

✳

skin health

✳

digestion support

✳

liver cleansing

LEMONS

Lemons are a big multi-tasker; in fact I can throw them at almost every health concern. They're helpful for anything skin, liver, immunity and heart related, thanks to the abundance of vitamin C and antioxidants, and are marvellous in the diets of anyone with asthma or at risk of stroke or cancer.

Many of the antioxidants in lemons are found in their yellow skin, and their absorption is helped by compounds found in the pith (the white part between the flesh and the outer skin). So make a tea with whole slices of lemon and honey (such as manuka), grate both the skin and pith into salads or gluten-free and refined sugar-free desserts, throw some unpeeled quarters in your next batch of roasted vegetables, squeeze lemon juice over any kind of soup just prior to serving. Lemons can be used in so many ways, both sweet and savoury.

Lemons contain B-group vitamins, beta-carotene, vitamin E, calcium, magnesium and potassium. A glass of tepid filtered water with the juice of half a lemon will aid digestion by way of increasing the hydrochloric acid levels in the stomach, helping to more effectively break down your food. This can be excellent as a part of the treatment of reflux, and for digestive complaints in general (note, though, that this is not recommended for those with stomach ulcers or an enflamed stomach lining). As a bitter tasting food, lemon is a great helper for the liver, increasing phase 2 detoxification, whereby toxins are on their way to being excreted by the body. This can have a major positive effect on many common ailments, including those inflammatory in nature like arthritis, skin conditions and hormonal imbalance.

Lemons are incredibly easy to incorporate into the regular diet by including a wedge of lemon with almost everything! It is surprisingly lovely squeezed over roast vegetables, salads, fish, chicken and lamb, and fruit salad. Lemons make for an incredibly hardy backyard fruiting tree, and grow almost anywhere with little or no maintenance once established, and have a really super-high yield. When you have a few up your sleeve, preserve 'em!

PRESERVED LEMONS

about 5 medium-sized lemons

¼ cup sea salt

1 cinnamon stick

3 star anise

5 black peppercorns

5 coriander seeds

5 cloves

1 bay leaf

Preserved lemons are a Moroccan staple and they're perfect plopped into a tagine or almost any kind of soup or stew, and gorgeous with roast lamb or chicken, or baked fish. They are brilliantly handy to have around, they take about 5 minutes to prepare, take all kinds of dishes into the stratosphere of deliciousness and if, like me, you have a lemon tree or two in the backyard, this is a fabulous way to make use of all your excess lemons.

Start by sterilizing your chosen jar. I use a medium-sized, 1 litre (2 pt) mason jar. Carefully place the jar and lid in a sink or bucket of boiling water, leave for 30 seconds and carefully remove (with tongs, oven mitts, tea towels, anything necessary to protect yourself from being scalded by the hot water) Allow the jar and lid to air-dry upside down on a clean tea towel.

Next, cut each lemon lengthways, almost into quarters, from the top down until you reach approximately 1 cm (⅓ in.) from the bottom. You should be able to gently open the lemon into a 4-petalled flower shape.

Wear rubber gloves while salting your lemons if you have any form of abrasion on your hands. This is both to make sure that the lemons remain sterile, but also to protect you from the burning nightmare that is salt and lemon juice into even the tiniest of wounds. In a bowl (to catch any extra salt), salt your lemons, ensuring every surface of the lemon is covered in salt. Rub and massage salt into both the inside and outside of your cut lemons. Next, put 1 tablespoon of salt into the bottom of the jar. Now, one by one, squash your lemons into the jar, layering in the star anise, peppercorns, coriander seeds, cloves and bay leaf. As you layer each lemon, use all the might of your thumbs to pack the lemons down; you want the salt to extract enough lemon juice to cover the lemons as they pickle for a month. Once all lemons are in, and are slightly covered in their own juice, leave a small air gap of at least 1 cm (⅓ in.) at the top of the jar, and screw on the lid. The jar should be airtight.

Once prepared, allow the jar to sit in a cool, dark place for around a month. Give the lemon a little rinse under running water immediately prior to use.

8. Herbs & Spices

Herbs and spices are what set different cuisines apart, and are the highly evocative taste profiles that form a crucial part of making eating a wholly sensory experience. From 'warming' ginger to 'cooling' mint and hot, pungent chilli, herbs and spices not only make eating interesting and enjoyable, they carry extraordinary nutrients and health properties. Experiment daily with different herbs and spices to make your food abundantly yummier, while also positively influencing your health while you're at it.

GINGER

Anyone who juices on a regular basis knows that a little ginger in the juice creates a powerful, inimitable *zing* that wakes you allll the way up. If you don't love ginger, start small and work your way up. There are a million and one dishes I can think of that would absolutely not be the same without ginger. If you regularly eat ginger, you're doing your body a great deal of wondrous good. Ginger is *powerful*, man. It has science in its corner. Studies have shown ginger to be a strong remedy for nausea (the old wives' tales were correct), including sea sickness and morning sickness, as well as hyperemesis gravidarum (extreme morning sickness).

Ginger is loaded with the active compound gingerol, which has been shown to ease menstrual cramps, reduce digestive discomfort and bloating and stave off bacterial infections. If that isn't impressive enough, gingerol has also been studied in relation to the treatment of cancer with promising results, and is an important inclusion in the diet of those with metabolic disorder and/or diabetes, as it has been shown to reduce blood sugar levels and heart disease risk factors like unbalanced cholesterol levels.

Aside from gingerol, ginger also contains magnesium, vitamin B6, vitamin C and fibre, and is also powerfully anti-inflammatory. It is commonly used topically as a poultice on painful arthritic joints and internally for various inflammatory conditions.

JAPANESE CARROT AND GINGER DRESSING

1 knob ginger (approximately 3–4 cm/ 1–1 ⅛ in.)

1 carrot

¼ onion, peeled and chopped

2 tablespoons unfiltered apple cider vinegar

3 tablespoons sesame oil

3 tablespoons extra virgin olive oil

1 tablespoons miso paste (contains gluten)

pinch of salt

1 spring onion (scallion)

MAKES APPROXIMATELY 1 CUP

Place all ingredients, except the spring onion, in a food processor and blend until very well combined and smooth. Slowly add tiny amounts of water if needed (1 teaspoon at a time) to help the ingredients combine.

Finely slice the spring onion and add to the dressing as a garnish. Serve over leafy greens.

OREGANO

Oregano is another of the helpful herbs that go wild in the garden with very little attention. Once established, they will go crazy, so keep in a pot to keep your sanity!

The soft, fragrant leaves of the oregano plant not only pep up a huge range of European and South American dishes, they're really handy to have around for a whole range of medicinal applications. If you're in the thick of wintertime cold and flu season, steep some fresh, bruised oregano leaves in boiling water for a few minutes and enjoy as a tea. Oregano is widely acknowledged for its antimicrobial and anti-inflammatory properties thanks to its various active compounds that also provide oregano's unique scent and flavour. Just the thing for a sore, irritated throat. Those same anti-inflammatory and antibacterial properties make oregano a fabulous tincture for a topical application for acne.

Oregano is rich in vitamin K, fibre, manganese, calcium, vitamin E and some omega-3 fatty acids, and is fantastic simply chopped and included in a garden salad. It contains compounds like limonene (insect repellant), thymol (highly antiseptic), pinene (antibacterial) and caryophyllene (anti-inflammatory).

Oregano is easy to incorporate into the diet regularly in the form of Chimichurri, the magical Argentinian sauce that adds a special something to most savoury dishes.

CHIMICHURRI

¾ cup oregano leaves

¾ cup parsley
(flat-leaf works best but
any will do)

3 cloves garlic, peeled

2–3 tablespoons unfiltered
apple cider vinegar or
lemon juice

½ cup extra virgin olive oil

sea salt, pepper and chilli
flakes, to taste

MAKES APPROXIMATELY 1½ CUPS

Place the herbs and garlic in a food processor and blend until finely
chopped and combined. With the food processor still running, slowly
add all other ingredients and blend until combined. Store in an airtight
container, but serve at room temperature (the oil component will
solidify in the fridge). Serve as a salad dressing, as a marinade on any
kind of meat or roast vegetables.

TURMERIC

If you are looking for a powerful anti-inflammatory then look no further, you've found it. It's turmeric (dubbed 'nature's anti-inflammatory' for good reason) and its active compound, curcumin. It is what colours your curry, detoxes your liver and alleviates inflammation within the body. What a crafty little friend to have on your side.

Turmeric contains manganese (which is anti-inflammatory and also good for joint health, so if you're arthritic, then turmeric is a double-whammy), iron, vitamin B6 and fibre. However, turmeric's crowning glory is its curcumin, which is the very thing that gives turmeric its bright yellow colour. Curcumin has been shown to be as effective as pharmacological anti-inflammatories, but without side-effects. It is a great tool in the defense against cancer, particularly colon cancer thanks to its antioxidant nature, and is a huge help to the detoxification process of the liver by increasing the liver's detoxification enzymes. Curcumin is effective in the management of some cardio, respiratory and neurological disorders as well, and I love to give it to clients who are experiencing hormonal imbalance (shout out to the menopausal/PCOS — Polycystic Ovary Syndrome — women of this world!) for its liver-boosting properties to aid the clearance of hormones and alleviate some balance-related symptoms.

The recipe for Turmeric Milk on the opposite page is just the ticket to warm up the tummy on a cold night, and the benefits are enormous, no matter if you're in perfect health, or are treating an ailment.

TURMERIC MILK

1–2 teaspoons ground or freshly grated turmeric

1–2 teaspoons ground cinnamon

1 teaspoon dried ground ginger

pinch of ground black pepper

1 tablespoon honey

2 cups unsweetened coconut milk or almond milk

2 sticks of cinnamon, to serve

Anti-inflammatory perfection in a cup! This is a wonderful, warming nightcap before bed, but you might be wondering why on earth I'd go around throwing pepper in a dang nightcap. It's there for a very good reason: black pepper contains piperine, an active compound which drastically increases the bioavailability of curcumin from turmeric, meaning it helps your body to absorb it. A pinch is enough, and flavour-wise it adds its own barely detectable warmth to this calmative mug. Be careful with bench tops, fingers, bleached blonde hair and clothes when preparing this drink, as it will stain whatever it comes in contact with.

SERVES 2

Place all ingredients into a small saucepan and simmer over a low heat for about 10 minutes until warmed through. Serve warm with a cinnamon stick as a stirrer.

CHILLI (CHILI PEPPERS)

There are two kinds of people in this world: those who dig chilli (chili peppers), and those who most definitely do not. I am most definitely in the former camp, liberally adding this spicy member of the nightshade family to breakfasts, lunches and dinners.

There are around 3000 different cultivated varieties of the chilli and as many different dishes in which to put them, and why not, since they not only have different flavours, they are unique in their range of health properties, including vitamin E, vitamin C (when eaten raw), vitamin A precursors, vitamin K, B-group vitamins (particularly B6), fibre and even a little plant-based iron.

Chillies are powerfully anti-inflammatory thanks to the active compound capsaicin, which has been found to inhibit inflammatory processes throughout the body, from skin conditions to various forms of arthritis. They are wonderfully decongestant so will help clear the overproduction of the mucous membranes, while boosting the immune system when you have a cold. A lovely big dose of fresh chillies added to a chicken and vegetable soup is a powerful elixir when battling a cold.

Regular consumption of chillies has not only been proven to reduce inflammation, but also to reduce blood cholesterol and triglycerides (especially for those suffering from metabolic syndrome and/or diabetes) as well as the incidence of blood clots. Chillies are also a great helping hand for those managing their weight, as chillies have been shown to increase the metabolic rate by reducing the body's requirements for insulin in order to metabolize carbohydrates.

Chillies are antioxidant and a spice I consider to be amongst the anti-ageing bag of edible tricks. Most varieties are very easy to grow in full sun or part shade and are great producers. I am lucky to grow a mix of red and green (same variety; the red has just been allowed to mature), bright orange and very hot habaneros, and beautiful shiny, black chillies to include in most of my cooking. Aside from their abundant health properties, chillies also add a beautiful visual element when used as a garnish. They will happily grow in a pot in a warm sunny spot if you are short on garden space, and tolerance for the heat of chillies can definitely be learned, so start mild and work your way up!

BAJAN SEASONING

4 cloves garlic

1 knob ginger

3 habanero or similar hot chillies (bird's eye and scotch bonnets work, too); use half a milder long red chilli (chili pepper) if you are building your tolerance, and remove the seeds if you are a bona fide chilli beginner

juice of 2 limes, plus extra for garnish

1 small bunch spring onions (scallions), green part only, chopped

small bunch of thyme

1 tablespoon ground allspice

Bajan Seasoning is perfect as a rub or marinade for sustainably caught fish (both fillets and whole) and on pastured organic chicken. This seasoning keeps well in the refrigerator for up to a week.

MAKES APPROXIMATELY 1 CUP

In a food processor, blend all the ingredients until a paste forms.

A lovely side salad for this recipe would be the radish salad on page 46 (see Fish Tacos with Radish Salad).

MINT

One of the iconic flavours of summer, mint is the cooling, refreshing herb our digestive systems need. It is fabulous in both sweet and savoury dishes, and grows like mad in the garden; in fact, you want to keep this baby contained in a pot since it throws out runners and can quickly (within a matter of weeks) overrun your entire garden if left unchecked. Like most herbs, the more you pick and eat, the more it thrives, so use it often: on top of a fruit salad, in fact, on top of any kind of salad, with lamb, in smoothies and juices, as a tea (hot or cold) in a sublime sorbet or on its own (I love chewing on a fresh sprig of the chocolate mint variety to stave off bad breath as I'm running out the door).

Mint is famously fantastic for digestion as it stimulates the salivary glands, encouraging the production of digestive enzymes to help break down food in the first stage of digestion in the mouth. It is antiseptic and antibacterial, and (along with cinnamon) is the herb of choice for oral hygiene, as well as acting as a decongestant when fighting a cold. A little diluted mint essential oil applied to the temples will soothe a raging headache, while a couple of drops sprinkled into a tepid bath will soothe sunburn and fever. The wonderful, distinct smell of mint can help mental concentration, ease nausea and fatigue.

REFRESHING MINT MOJITO POPS

2 cups filtered water

3 tablespoons raw honey

zest of 1–2 limes, finely grated

1 cup mint leaves, finely chopped

¼ cup lime juice

MAKES 6 ICEBLOCKS
(POPSICLES/ICE LOLLIES)

Place the water and honey in a saucepan over a medium heat and gently heat until combined, stirring until the honey is completely dissolved. Take off the heat and allow to cool. Add the lime zest, mint leaves and lime juice, stir thoroughly, or even blend with an electric hand mixer to fully combine all ingredients. Pour the mojito mixture into silicone iceblock (popsicle/ice lolly) molds and freeze overnight.

the benefits

anti-inflammatory

✻

*great for diabetics and
those with hormone
conditions*

✻

lowers cholesterol

✻

immune support

CINNAMON

Cinnamon is the warm, woody scented inner bark of either the Cassia Cinnamon tree (most commonly available) or the Ceylon Cinnamon tree (rarer, and higher in medicinal properties). Cinnamon is highly versatile; it will add warmth and depth to curries, will take a hot chocolate to brand-new levels of amazingness and is glorious in most desserts, adding sweetness to refined-sugar-free recipes.

I first started regularly using cinnamon in my cooking when first learning about Polycystic Ovarian Syndrome and its relation to insulin resistance (it is similar to but not as dire as diabetes). Cinnamon has been proven to reduce insulin resistance in those with diabetes. It is a fantastic addition to the diets of those afflicted with Metabolic Syndrome or those trying to control their weight as it encourages the uptake and utilization of sugar in the bloodstream. It is very high in anti-inflammatory antioxidants, and also has a reductive effect on LDL cholesterol in the bloodstream, and is fantastic at fighting bacterial and fungal infections. Cinnamon, when mixed with drinks, also forms a mucilaginous gel, similar to that of slippery elm bark, which is very soothing to the digestive tract.

RAW VEGAN CINNAMON AND CHOCOLATE CAKE

NOTE: OVERNIGHT SOAKING TIME REQUIRED

BASE

1½ cups raw almonds

1 cup pitted dates, soaked in warm water for 15 minutes

½ cup cacao powder

⅓ cup coconut oil

4 teaspoons vanilla paste

1 teaspoon ground cinnamon

optional: 8 teaspoons maple syrup

FILLING

4 cups raw cashews

8 Earl Grey teabags

⅓ cup cacao

1 cup pitted dates, soaked in warm water for 15 minutes

1 cup coconut oil

1 tablespoon vanilla paste

2 heaped teaspoons cinnamon

Soak the cashews by covering with 5 cups of warm (not hot) water, and add 5the teabags. Leave to soak overnight.

The next day, start by making the base. Place the almonds in a food processor and blend, then add all the remaining base ingredients one by one and blend until mixture is well combined and forms a firm ball when rolled between the fingers. Grease and line a springform cake tin with baking paper. Remove the base mixture from the food processor and press firmly into the base of the cake tin, then refrigerate for 30 minutes.

Meanwhile, make the filling. Drain the cashews, reserving the teabags and approximately 1 cup of the soaking liquid. Place the cashews in the food processor, along with the reserved liquid and the tea leaves from the teabags, then blend until smooth. Add all other ingredients and process until very well combined and smooth.

Remove the base from the refrigerator and spread the filling over the base, then return to the refrigerator for at least 3 hours.

BASIL

Basil's unique perfume is enough to elicit seriously strong love feelings in me. I adore everything about the different varieties, from the incredible fresh green hue of sweet basil, to the slightly peppery/minty taste and aubergine-coloured stalks of Thai basil. All types of basil are frightfully easy to grow at home, and to that end, please be careful as they will grow like wildfire if left to their own devices! If you don't wish to consume a lot of basil, grow yours in a pot; however if, like me, you like it in almost everything from salads to soups to burgers, then let it grow abundantly. It's one of those herbs that simply requires a little watering every now and again, and the more you pick it, the more it grows.

Aside from its powerful sniffing goodness, basil also has a lot of nutritional goodness. Abundant in vitamin K, which is heart, bone and cell protectant, manganese for joint health plus a little vitamin A and vitamin C, basil's real superpower is thanks to its antioxidant flavonoids, which have further cell protectant properties, and its volatile oils (the source of its gorgeous scent) which provide anti-inflammatory and antibacterial action, even against some strains of antibiotic-resistant bacteria.

BASIL AND WATERMELON GRANITA

5–6 cups cubed ripe watermelon

1 cup loosely packed basil leaves, finely chopped

1 egg white, at room temperature

¼ cup lime or lemon juice

SERVES 6

NOTE: I LIKE MY GRANITA EXTRA BASIL-Y; ADJUST QUANTITIES TO SUIT YOUR TASTE

Place all the ingredients into a food processor, or a jug if you prefer to use a stick blender. Blend until well combined. Pour the mixture into a shallow dish (not a deep bowl as it will freeze inconsistently. A casserole dish is great) and pop into the freezer for 3 or 4 hours.

Scoop out and serve on a hot day.

the benefits

brain health

✳

immune support

✳

blood cleanser

✳

skin health

✳

heart health

GARLIC

Garlic is one of the great multi-tasking foods that is fabulous for so many ailments, and takes lots of savoury foods to the next level of flavourfulness. I eat it on an almost daily basis in its cooked, dried and raw forms, and while it is true that strangers aren't exactly lining up to kiss me, bad breath is a very small price to pay for the potent antimicrobial, antifungal, antioxidant sulphuric compound that is allicin. This compound is the cause of the interesting mouth smells but also of strong immune systems, glowing complexions, healthy hearts and regulated blood pressures.

Garlic is high in manganese, making it a fantastic addition to the diet of anyone who suffers with joint issues. It is high in vitamin C, which, in conjunction with allicin, is a 1-2 punch against viruses and bacteria trying to make a home in your body. This combination also increases your skin cell turnover while inhibiting bacterial overgrowth from within if you suffer from acne, making for gorgeous skin. (Bear in mind that the vitamin C content is only present when garlic is eaten raw, as vitamin C is destroyed by the heat of the cooking process, and allicin is most potent when garlic is chopped, then left for a few minutes and eaten raw. A great way to eat chopped raw garlic is in a simple salad dressing).

Studies have demonstrated that regular consumption of garlic can reduce the number of colds a person will contract in a year, and also shortens the duration of a cold once it is has taken hold of you.

Garlic is an essential component in the diet of people who suffer from heart disease, high blood pressure and high cholesterol (often these conditions present in conjunction with each other) as it has been shown time and time again to regulate high LDL cholesterol levels, consistently reduce high blood pressure and reduce the oxidative pressures of the ageing process through its antioxidant compounds.

Garlic also acts as a chelator of heavy metals in the blood of people regularly exposed to industrial chemicals. High levels of heavy metals in the blood are thought to contribute to neurological disorders like Alzheimer's and Parkinson's diseases. Compounds found in garlic bind to heavy metals in the bloodstream, making it easier for the body to capture and excrete. Garlic has a big reputation as an all-round 'blood-cleaner' as it mops up stray viral components and bacteria, and this action, coupled with its sulphuric compounds, gives the liver a big helping hand as it goes about its business as the filter for our bodies.

GARLICKY GREENS

1 tablespoon coconut oil or extra virgin olive oil

3–4 cups green sautéing vegetables, roughly chopped e.g. broccolini, bok choy (pak choy), spinach, brussels sprouts, kale, silverbeet (Swiss chard)

2–3 cloves garlic, thinly sliced

dried chilli flakes (if desired)

sesame oil, sesame seeds and lemon juice, to serve

This recipe is side dish heaven and a delicious way to tempt those not overly sold on the taste of green vegetables.

SERVES 1–2 AS A SIDE

Place a large frying pan or wok over a high heat and add the coconut oil. Add all the greens, and sauté until half cooked, or when ever so slightly wilted. Add the garlic and chilli flakes, cook for another minute or two, then remove from the heat.

Serve with a little splash of sesame oil, lemon juice, and a sprinkling of sesame seeds. This side dish is insanely quick and easy, and is a great way to make green vegetables a much-desired addition to the dinner plate.

FENNEL SEEDS

Sweet-toothed people rejoice, for here is a friend from the spice family to hold your hand through your mid-afternoon sugar cravings. The seeds of the fennel plant are a wonderfully sweet, licorice-flavoured spice that offer a wealth of nutritional benefit, too.

Very high in insoluble fibre, fennel seeds are fabulous to aid constipation, as well as helping to balance cholesterol levels and reduce the likelihood of bowel (and other) cancers.

Though we typically only eat small amounts of fennel seeds at a time, they offer a great big mineral-containing bang for your buck, with iron, selenium, copper, calcium, manganese and magnesium.

DIGESTIVE FENNEL TEA

1 tablespoon fennel seeds

1 teaspoon ground ginger

1 teaspoon dried mint

After all that, I thought it best to finish with a calming digestive, utilizing the soothing properties of fennel seeds. All of the ingredients are commonly available in the spice section of the supermarket.

SERVES 1

Crush the fennel seeds in a mortar and pestle (or with the back of a tablespoon) to release the volatile oil and licorice flavour. Place all ingredients either directly in the cup or in a tea infuser, then cover with boiling water and allow to steep for at least 5 minutes. Enjoy after each meal to aid digestion and calm the nerves (caffeine free).

BIBLIOGRAPHY

Angelino, D. and Jeffery, E. 2014, 'Glucosinolate hydrolysis and bioavailability of resulting isothiocyanates: Focus on glucoraphanin', *Journal of Functional Foods*, 7, pp. 67–76, accessed 8 May 2016.

Bahadoran, Z., Mirmiran, P. and Azizi, F. 2013, 'Potential efficacy of broccoli sprouts as a unique supplement for management of Type 2 Diabetes and its complications', *Journal of Medicinal Food*, 16,5, accessed 9 May 2016.

Douglas, R.M. et al. 2005, 'Vitamin C for preventing and treating the common cold (meta-analysis)', *PLOS Medicine*, 2, 6, accessed 8 May 2016.

Eby, G.A. and Eby, K.L. 2006, 'Rapid recovery from major depression using magnesium treatment', *Medical Hypotheses*, 67, 2, pp. 362–70, accessed 8 May 2016.

Eid, N. et al. 2014, 'Polyphenols, glucosinolates, dietary fibre and colon cancer: Understanding the potential of specific types of fruit and vegetables to reduce bowel cancer progression', *Journal of Nutrition and Aging*, 2, 1, pp. 45–67, accessed 8 May 2016.

El-Sayed, A. et al. 2013, 'Dietary sources of lutein and zeaxanthin carotenoids and their role in eye health', *Nutrients*, 5, 4, accessed 8 May 2016.

Fujii, S. et al. 2015, 'Systematic synthesis and anti-inflammatory activity of --carboxylated menaquinone derivatives: Investigations on identified and putative vitamin K2 metabolites', *Bioorganic & Medicinal Chemistry*, 23, 10, pp. 2344–52, accessed 8 May 2016.

Gonzalez-Vallinas, M. et al. 2013, 'Dietary phytochemicals in cancer prevention and therapy: A complementary approach with promising perspectives', *Nutrition Reviews*, 71, 9, pp. 585–99, accessed 9 May 2016.

Holzapfel, N. et al. 2013, 'The potential role of lycopene for the prevention and therapy of prostate cancer: From molecular mechanisms to clinical evidence', *International Journal of Molecular Sciences*, 14, 7, accessed 9 May 2016.

Hullar, M.A., Burnett-Hartman, A.N. and Lampe, J.W. 2014, 'Gut microbes, diet, and cancer', *Advances in Nutrition and Cancer*, 6, pp. 377–99, accessed 8 May 2016.

Jacka, F.N. et al. 2009, 'Association between magnesium intake and depression and anxiety in community-dwelling adults: The Hordaland Health Study', *Australian and New Zealand Journal of Psychiatry*, 43, 1.

Korantzopoulos, P. et al. 2005, 'Oral vitamin C administration reduces early recurrence rates after electrical cardioversion of persistent atrial fibrillation and attenuates associated inflammation', *International Journal of Cardiology*, 102, 2, pp. 321–6.

Lappe, J. et al. 2015, 'The longitudinal effects of physical activity and dietary calcium on bone mass accrual across stages of pubertal development', *Journal of Bone and Mineral Research*, 30, 1, pp. 156–64, accessed 8 May 2016.

Lietz, G. et al. 2012, 'Single nucleotide polymorphisms upstream from the B-carotene 15,15'-monoxygenase gene influence provitamin A conversion efficiency in female volunteers', *Journal of Nutrition*, 142, 1.

Ma, L. and Lin, X.M. 2010, 'Effects of lutein and zeaxanthin on aspects of eye health', *Journal of the Science of Food and Agriculture*, 90, 1.

Oh, H.A. et al. 2016, 'Evaluation of the effect of kaempferol in a murine allergic rhinitis model', *European Journal of Pharmacology*, 718, 1–3, pp. 48–56, accessed 9 May 2016.

Sarah, M.H. et al. 2015, 'Recommendations for dietary calcium intake and bone health: The role of health literacy', *Journal of Nutrition and Food Sciences*, 6, 1.

Siervo, M. et al. 2013, 'Inorganic nitrate and beetroot juice supplementation reduces blood pressure in adults: A systematic review and meta-analysis', *Journal of Nutrition*, 143, 6.

Won An, Y. et al. 2016, 'Sulforaphane exerts its anti-inflammatory effect against amyloid-B peptide via STAT-1 dephosphorylation and activation of Nrf2/HO-1 cascade in human THP-1 macrophages', *Neurobiology of Aging*, 38, pp. 1–10, accessed 9 May 2016.

Wu, Q.J. et al. 2013, 'Cruciferous vegetable consumption and gastric cancer risk: A meta-analysis of epidemiological studies', *Cancer Science*, 104, 8, pp. 1067–73.

Zeng, H., Cao, J. and Combs, G. 2013, 'Selenium in bone health: Roles in antioxidant protection and cell proliferation', *Nutrients*, 5, 1, pp. 97–110, accessed 8 May 2016.

Zosky, G.R. et al. 2011, 'Vitamin D deficiency causes deficits in lung function and alters lung structure', *American Thoracic Society Journal*, 183, 10.

Zu, K. et al. 2014, 'Dietary lycopene, angiogenesis, and prostate cancer: A prospective study in the prostate-specific antigen era', *Journal of the National Cancer Institute*, accessed 9 May 2016.

ACKNOWLEDGMENTS

I would like to first acknowledge my incredible clients, who are encouraging and strong and wonderful beyond measure and truly support me as much as I support them. Each of you has been instrumental in my development as a nutritionist and I am hugely thankful for our catch-ups. You've all taught me so very much.

I would of course also like to thank my publisher Anouska Jones, Karen Gee and all of the exceptional team at Exisle Publishing. You have facilitated the realization of something I had always dreamed of but had never thought possible, and your excellent feedback, encouragement, enormous patience and hard work to get this book off the ground has been overwhelmingly wonderful. You're all magical wizards.

On a personal note, I thank my partner Troy for his unconditional love, support and patience with me during the writing of this book. Unhelpfully, his constructive criticism was non-existent: he loves everything I cook. But his unwavering tolerance of me over these last years has to be commended. Thank you.

Also, special thanks to my mother Susan and brothers Keaton and Nathan for their emotional support, feedback and long telephone calls. You're magnificent human beings and I feel lucky every day to have you all in my lives.

RECIPE INDEX

INDEX

LE CORDON BLEU

HOME COLLECTION

SEAFOOD

bay books

contents

 *easy* *a little more care needed* *more care needed*

Lobster bisque

Smooth, creamy bisques are thought to have Spanish origins, where in the province of Biscay they may originally have been made with pigeons or quail until shellfish took over as the main ingredient in the seventeenth century.

Preparation time **30 minutes**
Total cooking time **30 minutes**
Serves 4

1 large or 2 small uncooked lobsters,
   about 700–800 g (1 lb 7 oz–1 lb 10 oz) in total
2 tablespoons olive oil
¹/2 carrot, cut into cubes
¹/2 onion, cut into cubes
¹/2 small celery stick, cut into cubes
2¹/2 tablespoons brandy
150 ml (5 fl oz) dry white wine
4 large tomatoes, peeled, seeded and quartered
   or 50 g (1³/4 oz) passata
1 bouquet garni (see Chef's tip)
1.5 litres fish stock
85 g (2³/4 oz) rice flour
2 egg yolks
1 tablespoon thick (double) cream
1 teaspoon finely chopped fresh tarragon

1 If you have bought live lobsters, kill them according to the method in the Chef's techniques on page 61. If you prefer not to do this, ask your fishmonger to do it.
2 Prepare the lobster following the method in the Chef's techniques on page 61. Heat the oil in a large pan, add the lobster pieces in their shell and stir for 2 minutes over high heat. Add the carrot, onion and celery, reduce the heat and cook for 2 minutes. Add the brandy and immediately ignite at arm's length, then allow the flames to subside or cover with a lid. Pour in the wine and stir to blend in any sticky juices from the pan base. Add the tomato or passata, bouquet garni and stock and bring to the boil.
3 Using a slotted spoon, remove the lobster pieces from the stock, roughly break into small pieces using a knife and return to the pan with the rice flour. Stir to combine, bring to the boil and simmer for 10 minutes.
4 Pass the soup through a fine sieve, pressing the solids with the back of a spoon to extract all the juices, then discard the contents of the sieve, pour the liquid into a clean pan and season with salt and black pepper. The bisque should just coat the back of a spoon. If not, bring to the boil and simmer to reduce.
5 In a bowl, mix the egg yolks and cream together, stir in about 125 ml (4 fl oz) of the hot bisque, then pour back into the bisque. Check the seasoning and reheat for 5 minutes, stirring continuously, without boiling. Sprinkle over the tarragon and serve in warm bowls or a soup tureen.

Chef's tip To make the bouquet garni, wrap the green part of a leek loosely around a bay leaf, a sprig of thyme, some celery leaves and a few stalks of parsley, then tie with string. Leave a long tail to the string for easy removal.

Ceviche

Ceviche originated in South America and is the perfect way to show off the freshest fish. The acidity of the lime dressing magically 'cooks' the raw fish until it is opaque, just as if heat had been used.

Preparation time 55 minutes + 4 hours refrigeration
Total cooking time 1 minute
Serves 6

600 g (1¹/4 lb) bream, snapper or seabass fillets, skinned
   (see Chef's tips)
juice of 6 limes
1 small onion, finely chopped
1 green capsicum (pepper), halved, seeded and
   finely chopped
¹/2 red chilli, seeded and finely chopped
¹/2 cucumber, cut into 5 mm (¹/4 inch) cubes
1 small avocado, peeled and cut into 5 mm
   (¹/4 inch) cubes
4 tomatoes, peeled, seeded and diced
few sprigs of fresh parsley or chervil, to garnish

WATERCRESS VINAIGRETTE
100 g (3¹/4 oz) watercress, tough stems removed
1¹/4 tablespoons white wine vinegar
100 ml (3¹/4 fl oz) olive oil

1 Cut the bream, snapper or seabass fillets into 5 mm (¹/4 inch) wide slices, pour over the lime juice, cover and refrigerate for about 2 hours.

2 Drain the fish, then add some salt and black pepper, the onion, capsicum, chilli, cucumber and avocado and mix gently to combine. Cover with plastic wrap and refrigerate for 1–2 hours. Chill six serving plates.

3 To make the watercress vinaigrette, add the watercress to a pan of boiling salted water and cook for about 1 minute, then drain and run under cold water. Pat dry with paper towels to remove excess water, then purée in a blender or food processor with the white wine vinegar and olive oil. Season with some salt and black pepper.

4 To serve, place an 8 cm (3 inch) pastry cutter in the centre of a chilled plate and spoon the ceviche into it until full, packing down lightly with the back of a spoon. Remove the cutter and repeat on the other plates. Decorate the plates with the watercress vinaigrette and garnish with the diced tomato and parsley or chervil. Serve with some crusty bread.

Chef's tips If you can only buy a whole bream, snapper or seabass, buy an 800 g (1 lb 10 oz) fish and fillet it yourself (see Chef's techniques, page 63).

For a more creamy variation to this dish, add 250 ml (8 fl oz) coconut milk with the vegetables.

Gravlax

A Scandinavian method of curing salmon in salt, sugar and dill. The salmon is left to marinate for 1¹/₂ days and is then served with a traditional sweet dill and mustard dressing.

Preparation time **1 hour + 36 hours refrigeration**
Total cooking time **Nil**
Serves 10

1.8 kg (3 lb 10 oz) salmon fillet, skin on
but scales removed
115 g (3³/4 oz) rock or sea salt
85 g (2³/4 oz) caster sugar
4 tablespoons chopped fresh dill
1¹/2 tablespoons black peppercorns, crushed
2 teaspoons coriander seeds, crushed
1 teaspoon ground mixed spice
6 tablespoons roughly chopped fresh dill leaves

DILL AND MUSTARD DRESSING
2 teaspoons sweet mustard (German) or 2 teaspoons
grain mustard mixed with 2 teaspoons honey
2 teaspoons chopped fresh dill
2 teaspoons white wine vinegar or cider vinegar
220 ml (7 fl oz) vegetable oil

1 Wash the salmon, dry it with paper towels and lay on a tray or plate, skin-side-down. Mix together the salt, sugar, dill, peppercorns, coriander seeds and mixed spice and spoon it over the fish. Cover with plastic wrap, place a baking tray on top and a roughly 500 g (1 lb) weight to lightly press the salmon (this could be cans spaced out along the fish). Refrigerate for 24 hours.

2 Remove the weights and covering, discard the solids from the marinade, then rinse the remaining marinade off with cold water and pat the salmon dry with paper towels. Place on a clean tray or plate, skin-side-down.

3 Press the dill leaves onto the salmon, then cover with plastic wrap and press well with your fingers to make the dill adhere. Refrigerate for 12 hours.

4 To make the dill and mustard dressing, mix all the ingredients except the oil together in a bowl with some salt and black pepper, then slowly drizzle the oil into the bowl, whisking to emulsify with the other ingredients.

5 Uncover the salmon, remove any excess dill, then lift onto a board. With a long, thin-bladed knife held at an angle of 45 degrees and about 6–8 cm (2¹/2–3 inches) from the tail, cut a slice towards the tail and continue slicing to produce short thin slices. Serve with the dressing.

Chef's tip For a variation, try this beetroot and mustard mixture. Follow the recipe to the end of Step 2, then combine 50 g (1³/4 oz) mustard seeds (soaked in cold water for 30 minutes, then drained) and 250 g (8 oz) very finely chopped cooked beetroot. Press onto the salmon and continue as above.

Gravlax (top) and Beetroot and mustard gravlax

Seafood paella

A classic Spanish dish consisting of rice and saffron, often combined with chicken, pork and chorizo, although here we use seafood only. The name is derived from the large two-handled dish in which the paella is traditionally cooked and served.

Preparation time **45 minutes**
Total cooking time **45 minutes**
Serves 4

3 pinches of saffron threads
3 tablespoons olive oil
I large onion, sliced
300 g (10 oz) long-grain rice
3 tomatoes, peeled, seeded and roughly chopped or 400 g (12³/4 oz) can chopped tomatoes, drained
2 cloves garlic, crushed
550 ml (18 fl oz) chicken or vegetable stock
300 g (10 oz) mussels, scrubbed and beards removed (see page 62)
16 large raw prawns, shells on
I cooked crab in its shell, cleaned and cut into quarters, or 4 cooked crab claws in their shells (see Chef's tips)
300 g (10 oz) small clams, cockles or pipi, well washed
150 g (5 oz) firm white fish fillets, skinned and cut into 3 cm (1¹/4 inch) pieces
90 g (3 oz) frozen baby peas
I red capsicum (pepper), cut into 2.5 cm (1 inch) lengths and thinly sliced

1 Place the saffron threads in a small bowl and soak in 2 tablespoons hot water.

2 Heat the oil in a paellera or heavy-based frying pan, 30–35 cm (12–14 inches) in diameter, add the onion and cook for about 3–4 minutes, or until soft. Add the rice and saffron and cook, stirring, for 2 minutes. Add the tomato, garlic and stock and bring to the boil. Reduce the heat and stir in half the mussels, prawns, crab, clams and fish with all the peas and red capsicum. Season well with salt and black pepper.

3 Arrange the remaining seafood on top and cover with a piece of greaseproof paper and a lid. Cook over low heat for 30 minutes, or until the rice is tender and the liquid has been absorbed. Don't stir the paella while it cooks as this will break up the fish and make the finished dish look messy. If the liquid has been absorbed but the rice is not cooked, add a little extra water and continue cooking until the rice is cooked through. Discard any unopened mussels and serve immediately.

Chef's tips Paella is traditionally served directly from the paellera or pan. If you are using a frying pan, check it is deep enough (3–5 cm/1¹/4–2 inches) to hold the liquid.

To clean a crab, remove the stomach sac and grey spongy fingers (gills).

Coquilles Saint-Jacques mornay

Coquilles Saint Jacques is the French term for scallops, meaning Saint James's shells. Here they are baked in the half shell and classically coated beneath piped potato and a Gruyère cheese sauce.

*Preparation time **25 minutes***
*Total cooking time **45 minutes***
Serves 4

8 large fresh scallops in their shells
55 g (1³/4 oz) Gruyère cheese, finely grated

DUCHESSE POTATOES
1 kg (2 lb) floury potatoes, peeled and cut
  into pieces
25 g (³/4 oz) unsalted butter
2 egg yolks
pinch of grated nutmeg

MORNAY SAUCE
15 g (¹/2 oz) unsalted butter
15 g (¹/2 oz) plain flour
250 ml (8 fl oz) milk
1 egg yolk
55 g (1³/4 oz) Gruyère cheese, grated

1 To prepare the scallops, follow the method in the Chef's techniques on page 62. Place the scallops flat on a board and slice each one into three circles, leaving the orange roe whole. Cover and refrigerate until needed.
2 Scrub the scallop shells and place in a pan of cold water, bring to the boil and simmer for 5 minutes. Drain and leave the shells to cool and dry.
3 To make the duchesse potatoes, place the potatoes in a large pan of salted, cold water. Cover and bring to the boil, then reduce the heat and simmer for 15–20 minutes, or until the potatoes are tender to the point of a sharp knife. Drain, return to the pan and shake over low heat for 1–2 minutes to remove excess moisture. Mash or push through a fine sieve into a bowl, then stir in the butter and egg yolks and season with nutmeg, salt and black pepper. Spoon the mixture into a piping bag with a 1.5 cm (5/8 inch) star nozzle. Preheat the oven to moderately hot 200°C (400°F/Gas 6).
4 To make the mornay sauce, melt the butter in a heavy-based pan over low-medium heat. Sprinkle over the flour and cook for 1 minute without allowing it to colour, stirring continuously with a wooden spoon. Remove from the heat and slowly add the milk, blending thoroughly. Return to the heat and bring slowly to the boil, stirring constantly. Lower the heat and cook for 3–4 minutes, or until the sauce coats the back of a spoon. Remove from the stove and stir in the egg yolk and cheese, then season with some salt and black pepper.
5 Pipe shell shapes or small overlapping circles of duchesse potato to form a border around the edge of each shell. Place on a baking tray with a rim so that the round edge of each shell rests on the rim to stop the filling running out. Place a sliced scallop and whole roe in each rounded shell, season with salt and black pepper and spoon over the mornay sauce. Sprinkle the cheese over the sauce and bake for about 12–15 minutes, or until golden brown.

Smoked trout pâté

A stylish but easy-to-make pâté, with a combination of fresh and smoked trout. For a variation, you could also use smoked and fresh salmon or mackerel.

*Preparation time **30 minutes + cooling + 1 hour refrigeration***
*Total cooking time **5 minutes***
Serves 6

1 tablespoon white wine vinegar
1 bay leaf
4 white peppercorns
115 g (3³/4 oz) fresh trout fillet, skin on
315 g (10 oz) smoked trout fillet, skinned
200 g (6¹/2 oz) cream cheese
100 g (3¹/4 oz) unsalted butter, softened
3 teaspoons fresh lemon juice
4 sprigs fresh parsley, chervil or dill, to garnish

1 Place the vinegar, bay leaf, peppercorns and 100 ml (3¹/4 fl oz) water in a shallow pan and bring slowly to simmering point. Place the fresh trout skin-side-down in this poaching liquid, cover and gently cook for about 3–4 minutes, or until cooked through. Allow to cool in the liquid. Using a fish slice or spatula, lift the trout onto a plate and remove and discard the skin and any bones.

2 Place the fresh and smoked trout in a food processor and process to a smooth purée. Add the cream cheese, butter, lemon juice and some salt and black pepper and process until all the ingredients are thoroughly combined. Divide the pâté among six 250 ml (8 fl oz) ramekins, about 8 cm (3 inches) in diameter, and place in the refrigerator for 1 hour. To serve, garnish with a sprig of parsley, chervil or dill and accompany with Melba toast.

Chef's tip This makes an excellent cocktail dip if served soft at cool room temperature. Alternatively, pipe it onto small rounds of toast as a canapé and garnish with a sprig of dill or chervil.

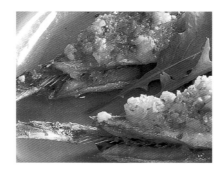

Sardines with walnut and parsley topping

A crisp walnut topping gives these grilled fresh sardines a lovely texture. They can be served as a main course or appetizer with warm olive oil, lemon wedges, rocket leaves and plenty of fresh bread.

*Preparation time **40 minutes***
*Total cooking time **20 minutes***
Serves 4

WALNUT AND PARSLEY TOPPING
150 g (5 oz) unsalted butter
4 French shallots, finely chopped
2 cloves garlic, crushed
4 tablespoons fresh white breadcrumbs
110 g (3³/4 oz) walnuts, finely chopped
2 teaspoons finely chopped fresh parsley

16 x 50 g (1³/4 oz) fresh sardines,
scaled and gutted
2 tablespoons plain flour
50 ml (1³/4 fl oz) olive oil
2 tablespoons olive oil, warm, to serve
lemon wedges, to serve
a few rocket leaves, to serve

1 To make the walnut and parsley topping, melt the butter in a pan over moderate heat, add the shallots and garlic, cover and cook for about 3 minutes, or until soft and translucent. Remove from the stove, season with some salt and black pepper, then add the breadcrumbs, walnuts and parsley and mix thoroughly.

2 Preheat the grill to high. Wash the sardines, then dry well on paper towels. Place the flour on a plate or piece of greaseproof paper and season well with salt and black pepper. Pour the oil onto a separate plate. One at a time, roll the sardines in the flour to coat them, then shake off the excess flour. Dip into the oil, coating on both sides, then transfer half the sardines to the grill pan. Place under the grill and cook for 3 minutes on each side. Remove the first batch to a plate and keep warm while you cook the second batch.

3 Sprinkle the walnut and parsley topping over the sardines and press firmly onto the skin. Return to the grill, in two batches, and cook until the topping is golden brown.

4 Place the sardines on a large serving plate or individual plates and drizzle the warm olive oil around the sardines on the bare areas of the plate. Complete with some black pepper, the lemon wedges and a few rocket leaves.

Coulibiac

A Russian fish pie packed with salmon, rice, hard-boiled eggs and mushrooms, then wrapped in puff pastry to form a pillow shape. A great dish for a party, especially when served with warm beurre blanc.

*Preparation time **50 minutes + 15 minutes refrigeration***
*Total cooking time **1 hour 40 minutes***
Serves 8

55 g (1³/4 oz) long-grain rice
4 eggs
50 g (1³/4 oz) unsalted butter
6 small spring onions, finely sliced
3 large French shallots, finely chopped
400 g (12³/4 oz) mushrooms, finely chopped
juice of ¹/2 lemon
500 g (1 lb) salmon fillet, skin on
500 g (1 lb) ready-made puff pastry
2¹/2 tablespoons finely chopped fresh dill
1 egg yolk
100 g (3¹/4 oz) fromage fraîs or natural yoghurt

COURT BOUILLON
1 small carrot, roughly chopped
1 small onion, roughly chopped
1 bay leaf
4 fresh parsley stalks
1 sprig fresh thyme
6 black peppercorns
2 tablespoons white wine vinegar

1 Cook the rice until tender, then drain well. Hard-boil 3 of the eggs for 10 minutes, place in a bowl of iced water to cool quickly, then coarsely grate or finely chop.
2 Melt half the butter in a pan and add the spring onion. Cover and cook for 4 minutes over low heat until soft and translucent. Season and set aside.
3 Melt the remaining butter, add the shallots and cook gently for 2 minutes. Add the mushrooms, lemon juice, salt and pepper and cook until the mushrooms are dry.
4 To make the court bouillon, place all the ingredients except the vinegar in a pan with 1.5 litres water and a large pinch of salt. Bring to the boil, then simmer, covered, for 15 minutes. Add the vinegar and simmer for 5 minutes.
5 Add the salmon to the court bouillon and poach, covered, for 5 minutes. Remove from the heat, uncover and let the salmon cool in the liquid before transferring to a plate. Remove the flesh in large flakes from the skin and cover with plastic wrap. Discard any skin and bones.
6 Cut the pastry in half and, on a lightly floured surface, roll out one half to a 3 mm (¹/8 inch) thick rectangle. Transfer to a baking tray without a lip and trim down to a rectangle big enough to contain the salmon, about 23 x 35 cm (9 x 14 inches). Wrap and chill the trimmings, layering them flat. Leaving a 2.5 cm (1 inch) border on all sides, spread the rice in the centre of the pastry. Sprinkle over ¹/2 tablespoon of dill, then the salmon, salt and pepper, mushroom mixture, egg and spring onion in separate layers.
7 Beat the remaining egg and brush over the pastry border. Roll the remaining pastry to about 45 x 30 cm (18 x 12 inches), then pick the pastry up on the rolling pin and place over the filling. Press the edges together to seal the top and bottom, then trim neatly and brush with egg. Roll out the reserved trimmings and cut strips to decorate the pie. Lay them on as a lattice and place the pie in the refrigerator for 10–15 minutes.
8 Preheat the oven to moderately hot 200°C (400°F/ Gas 6). Beat the yolk and remaining egg together and brush over the pie. Wipe off any egg from the tray and make three small holes down the centre of the pie with a skewer. Bake for 30 minutes, until risen, crisp and golden.
9 Stir the remaining dill into the fromage fraîs or yoghurt and serve with slices of the Coulibiac.

Chef's tip For a special dinner, the coulibiac could be served with a beurre blanc sauce (see page 44).

Bouillabaisse

Fishermen in Marseille made this fragrant soup using fish that were difficult to sell. These were tossed into a simmering pot, hence the name Bouillabaisse, from 'bouillir' (to boil) and 'abaisser' (to reduce). You can use any combination of the fish below in the soup, and increase the amount of one fish if another is not available.

Preparation time 1 hour
Total cooking time 1 hour 10 minutes
Serves 4–6

1 John Dory, filleted and bones reserved (see page 63)
2 sole, filleted and bones reserved (see page 63)
500 g (1 lb) monkfish or ling, filleted and
  bones reserved (see page 62)
1 small sea bream, filleted and bones reserved
  (see page 62)
500 g (1 lb) conger eel, cut into pieces
90 ml (3 fl oz) olive oil
2 cloves garlic, finely chopped
pinch of saffron threads
1 carrot, fennel bulb and leek, white part only, cut into
  julienne strips (see Chef's tip)
24 thin slices French baguette, for croûtes
3 cloves garlic, cut in half, for croûtes
chopped fresh basil, to garnish

SOUP
1 small leek, onion and fennel bulb, sliced thinly
1 celery stick, sliced thinly
2 cloves garlic
2 tablespoons tomato paste
500 ml (16 fl oz) white wine
pinch of saffron threads
2 sprigs of fresh thyme
1 bay leaf
4 sprigs of fresh parsley

ROUILLE SAUCE
1 egg yolk
1 tablespoon tomato paste
3 cloves garlic, crushed into a paste

pinch of saffron threads
250 ml (8 fl oz) olive oil
1 baked potato, about 200 g (6¹/2 oz)

1 Season the fish and eel and toss with half the oil, the garlic, saffron, carrot, fennel and leek. Cover and refrigerate.
2 To make the soup, heat the remaining oil in a stockpot over high heat, add the reserved bones and cook for 3 minutes. Stir in the leek, onion, fennel, celery and garlic and cook for 2 minutes, then mix in the tomato paste and cook for 2 minutes. Pour in the wine and simmer for 5 minutes. Finally, add 1 litre water, the saffron and herbs and simmer for 20 minutes. Strain through a sieve, pressing down to extract as much juice as possible, then discard the solids. Place the soup in a pan and simmer for 15 minutes until slightly thickened, skimming to remove any foam that floats to the surface.
3 To make the rouille, whisk the egg yolk in a small bowl with the tomato paste, garlic, saffron and some salt and black pepper. Continue to whisk while slowly pouring the oil into the mixture. Press the flesh of the potato through a sieve and whisk into the sauce.
4 Lightly toast the French baguette under a preheated grill, cool, then rub both sides with the cut sides of the half cloves of garlic to make garlic croûtes. Set aside.
5 Cut each fish fillet into six and add to a large pot with the eel and julienne vegetables. Pour the hot soup over and simmer for 7 minutes, or until the fish is cooked. Remove the fish and vegetables and place in an earthenware or metal dish. Whisk three tablespoons of the rouille into the soup to thicken it a bit, then pour the soup over the fish and sprinkle with the basil. Serve with the garlic croûtes and the remaining rouille.

Chef's tip Julienne strips are strips of vegetables, the size and shape of matchsticks.

Garlic prawns

Ideal as an appetizer or light summer lunch, serve this Spanish-inspired dish with lots of crusty bread to soak up the lemony garlic butter.

*Preparation time **20 minutes***
*Total cooking time **10 minutes***
Serves 4

120 g (4 oz) endive or frisée
1 red chilli, seeded and very thinly sliced
1 tablespoon fresh chervil leaves
24 medium raw tiger or gamba prawns, shells on
2 teaspoons vegetable or olive oil
4 cloves garlic, crushed
125 g (4 oz) unsalted butter, cut into cubes
finely grated rind and juice of 1 lemon
1 tablespoon finely chopped fresh parsley

1 Mix together the endive or frisée, chilli and chervil leaves and pile onto the centre of four plates.

2 Shell and devein the prawns, removing the heads but leaving the tails intact, following the method in the Chef's techniques on page 60. Place the prawns on a plate and season lightly with salt and black pepper. Heat the oil in a large, heavy-based frying pan. Add the prawns and, over medium-high heat, fry for about 1 minute on each side, or until cooked through. Remove and keep warm.

3 Add the garlic to the pan and cook for 1 minute, then add the cubes of butter and cook for 4 minutes, or until the butter is nut brown. Remove from the stove and add the lemon rind and juice and the parsley.

4 Quickly shake the pan once or twice to combine all the ingredients, then add the prawns and toss briefly to warm through. Immediately arrange the prawns around the salad on the plates with any remaining pan juices poured over the top.

Whole baked salmon with watercress mayonnaise

Baked in foil to retain the salmon's flavour and moist texture, this impressive centrepiece is the perfect dish for a large summer gathering, served with new potatoes and summer vegetables.

*Preparation time **1 hour 10 minutes**
    + 1 hour refrigeration*
*Total cooking time **40 minutes***
Serves 10–12

**1.5–1.75 kg (3–3¹/2 lb) whole fresh salmon, cleaned
    and scaled (ask your fishmonger to gut the fish
    and remove the scales)**
1 small onion, thinly sliced
1 small bay leaf
1 sprig fresh thyme
5 fresh parsley stalks
90 ml (3 fl oz) dry white wine
sprigs of watercress, to garnish
lemon wedges, to garnish

WATERCRESS MAYONNAISE
120 g (4 oz) watercress, tough stems removed
315 g (10 oz) whole-egg mayonnaise
few drops of lemon juice

1 Lift up the gill flap behind the cheek of the salmon head and, using kitchen scissors, remove the dark, frilly gills. Repeat on the other side of the fish. If any scales remain, hold the tail and, using the back of a knife, scrape the skin at a slight angle, working towards the head. Trim the fins. Cut across the tail to shorten it by half, then cut a V shape into the tail. Wash the salmon under cold water and open it on the belly side where the fishmonger has slit it. Remove the blood vessel lying along the backbone using a spoon. Rinse and wipe inside and out with paper towels.

2 Preheat the oven to moderate 180°C (350°F/Gas 4). Butter a piece of foil large enough to wrap around the fish and place on a large baking tray. Lay the salmon just off centre and place the onion and herbs inside the belly. Season with salt and black pepper, then pour over the wine. Quickly cover with foil and seal the edges tightly.

3 Bake for 30–40 minutes, or until the fish feels springy and firm to the touch. Open the foil and leave to cool. Remove the flavourings and lift the salmon onto greaseproof paper, draining off any liquid. Prepare the salmon for serving following the Chef's techniques on page 63, then cover with plastic wrap and refrigerate for 1 hour, or until needed.

4 To make the watercress mayonnaise, add the watercress to a pan of boiling salted water and cook for 1 minute, then drain and run under cold water. Pat dry with paper towels to remove excess water, then purée in a blender or food processor. Beat the purée gradually into the mayonnaise. If it is too dry, add a few drops of lemon juice. Season with salt and black pepper.

5 To serve, decorate the fish with some mayonnaise and serve the remainder separately. Garnish with the watercress sprigs and lemon wedges.

American crab cakes

These crispy crab cakes make a perfect light lunch with salad, or you can make lots of small ones to serve as appetizers at a Fourth of July barbecue or as part of a summer picnic.

*Preparation time **55 minutes + 20 minutes cooling + 30 minutes refrigeration***
*Total cooking time **20 minutes***
Serves 4–6

2 tablespoons vegetable oil
I onion, finely chopped
2 cloves garlic, crushed
I 1/2 tablespoons grated fresh ginger
I small red capsicum (pepper), halved, seeded and
  cut into cubes
8 spring onions, finely chopped
480 g (15 oz) white crab meat,
  drained well if frozen
2 teaspoons Tabasco
2 tablespoons chopped fresh flat-leaf parsley
3 tablespoons fresh breadcrumbs
1/2 teaspoon Dijon mustard
I egg, beaten
200 g (6 1/2 oz) seasoned flour, sieved, for coating
100 g (3 1/4 oz) fresh breadcrumbs, for coating
60 g (2 oz) Parmesan, grated, for coating
2 eggs, beaten, for coating
oil, for deep-frying
lemon wedges, to serve

1 Heat the oil in a frying pan and add the onion, garlic and ginger. Cook for 1 minute, then add the capsicum and spring onion and cook for 2 minutes, or until soft. Transfer to a plate and leave for 20 minutes to cool completely. When cool, stir in the crab meat, Tabasco, parsley, breadcrumbs, mustard and some salt and black pepper. Add the egg and bind together.

2 Divide the mixture into 4, 6 or 12, depending on what size cakes you want. Using lightly floured hands and a lightly floured surface, shape into cakes. Place on a tray, cover and refrigerate for 30 minutes, or until firm.

3 Place the flour on a large piece of greaseproof paper. Combine the breadcrumbs and Parmesan on another piece of paper. Place the egg in a shallow dish. One at a time, place the cakes in the flour, then pat off any excess. Place in the egg and use a brush to help coat. Remove with a fish slice, place on the breadcrumbs and Parmesan and toss all over the cake. Reshape the cakes, pressing the crumbs firmly on, then place on a tray.

4 Heat a 1 cm (1/2 inch) depth of oil in a non-stick frying pan and cook the cakes, in batches, over medium heat for 1–2 minutes each side, or until golden. Drain on crumpled paper towels and serve with lemon wedges.

Chef's tip To keep the crab cakes warm and crisp, place on a wire rack in a warm oven.

Seafood risotto

In this recipe, baby clams, prawns, mussels, crab and red mullet provide a host of different textures and flavours set in a creamy saffron risotto. Any combination of fresh seafood could be used instead.

Preparation time **35 minutes**
Total cooking time **1 hour**
Serves 4

150 g (5 oz) baby clams
2 red mullet, about 220–250 g (7–8 oz) each, filleted and
  with skin on but scales removed (see page 63)
150 g (5 oz) raw prawns, shells on
200 ml (6¹/2 fl oz) dry white wine
5 tablespoons olive oil
I small onion, finely chopped
250 g (8 oz) mussels, scrubbed and beards removed (see
  page 62)
I bay leaf
I sprig of fresh thyme
500 ml (16 fl oz) fish stock
pinch of saffron threads
I clove garlic, finely chopped
250 g (8 oz) arborio rice
60 g (2 oz) Parmesan, grated
grated rind of I lime
1¹/2 tablespoons crème fraîche or sour cream
105 g (3¹/2 oz) white crab meat, drained well if frozen
few fresh basil leaves, to garnish

1 Scrub and rinse the clams under running water to get rid of grit, then discard any that are open or damaged. Trim the mullet, then pin bone it following the Chef's techniques on page 63. Shell and devein the prawns, reserving the heads and shells, following the method in the Chef's techniques on page 60.

2 Place the clams in a pan, add half the wine and cook, covered, for 3 minutes, or until they open. Drain through a sieve lined with damp paper towel and reserve the liquid. Discard any unopened clams, then remove the clams from their shells and cover. Discard the shells.

3 In a pan, heat a tablespoon of the oil, add half the onion and cook over low heat for 4 minutes, or until soft and transparent. Add the remaining wine, mussels, bay leaf and thyme and cook, covered, for 2–3 minutes, or until the mussels open. Drain as for the clams, reserving the liquid. Discard any unopened mussels, then remove from their shells and cover.

4 In a pan, place the stock, 500 ml (16 fl oz) water, the clam and mussel liquid, prawn heads and shells and saffron. Bring to the boil, simmer for 10 minutes, then strain through a fine sieve. Return to the rinsed pan and keep warm.

5 In a pan or flameproof casserole, heat a tablespoon of oil, add the garlic and remaining onion and cook over low heat for 2–3 minutes, or until soft. Add the rice and stir for 2 minutes with a wooden spoon, making sure it is completely coated with the oil, then pour in enough stock to just cover the rice. Cook over low heat, stirring continuously, until the stock is absorbed. Continue to cook for 15–20 minutes, pouring in a little stock and allowing it to be absorbed before adding more. The risotto is ready when the rice is just tender but still *al dente* (there should also be a little stock left over). Remove from the heat, fold in the Parmesan, lime rind and crème fraîche and cover. Reserve the remaining stock.

6 Meanwhile, preheat the grill and brush the fish with a little olive oil. Season with salt and black pepper and grill, skin-side-up, for 2 minutes. Cover and keep warm. Heat the remaining oil in a large pan and toss the prawns over high heat for 2 minutes, or until pink and cooked through.

7 Pour the remaining stock into a pan, add the mussels, clams and crab and just heat through. Mix the seafood and its liquid into the risotto and transfer to a serving dish. Place the mullet and basil on top.

Smoked haddock gougère

A cheese-flavoured crown of choux pastry here holds a filling of smoked haddock, leek, tomato and dill. For a variation, you could try a mixture of fish such as salmon, trout or monkfish, or perhaps some shellfish.

Preparation time **35 minutes**
Total cooking time **45 minutes**
Serves 6

CHOUX PASTRY
150 g (5 oz) plain flour
100 g (3¼ oz) unsalted butter, cut into cubes
pinch of salt
4 eggs, lightly beaten
100 g (3¼ oz) Cheddar, coarsely grated
1 teaspoon Dijon mustard

FILLING
310 g (10 oz) smoked haddock fillet
15 g (½ oz) unsalted butter
1 small leek or 4 spring onions, white part only, sliced
15 g (½ oz) plain flour
180 ml (5¾ fl oz) milk
*1 large tomato, peeled, seeded and cut into
    1 cm (½ inch) strips*
1 teaspoon chopped fresh dill

1 egg, beaten
1 tablespoon grated Parmesan
1 tablespoon lightly toasted fresh breadcrumbs
20 g (¾ oz) unsalted butter, melted
fresh dill, to garnish

1 Brush six 14.5 x 3 cm (5¾ x 1¼ inch) round gratin dishes with melted butter and refrigerate to set.
2 To make the choux pastry, sift the flour onto a clean sheet of greaseproof paper. Place 250 ml (8 fl oz) water, the butter and salt in a pan. Heat until the butter and water come to the boil. Remove from the heat and add the flour all at once, then mix well using a wooden spoon. Return to the heat and stir until a smooth ball forms and the dough leaves the sides of the pan, then remove from the heat and place the dough in a bowl. Using a wooden spoon or electric beaters, add the eggs to the dough a little at a time, beating well after each addition. The mixture is ready to use when it is smooth, thick and glossy. Beat in the cheese, mustard and season well with salt and black pepper. Cover and set aside.
3 To make the filling, place the smoked haddock flat in a shallow pan and pour in enough cold water to cover. Slowly bring to the boil, covered, then turn off the heat and leave for 7 minutes.
4 Melt the butter in a deep pan, add the leek and cook over low heat for 3 minutes to soften. Sprinkle over the flour, stir in using a wooden spoon and cook for 1 minute. Remove from the heat, mix in the milk, then return to the heat and bring to the boil, stirring continuously. Simmer for 1 minute, or until the mixture thickens.
5 Preheat the oven to moderately hot 200°C (400°F/ Gas 6). Lift the fish from its cooking liquid, pat dry with paper towels, then use a fork to lightly take the fish off its skin in flakes. Gently stir the flakes into the filling with the tomato, dill and some salt and black pepper.
6 Fill a piping bag with a 1–1.25 cm (½–⅝ inch) nozzle with the pastry. Pipe a circle around the outside of the base of the prepared dishes, then a second circle on top to cover the side of the dish. Spoon the filling into the middle of the choux circles and brush the top of the pastry lightly with the beaten egg. Combine the Parmesan and breadcrumbs, sprinkle over the filling, then drizzle with the melted butter. Place on a baking tray and bake for 15–20 minutes, or until the pastry is risen and crisp. Sprinkle with dill to garnish.

Chef's tips You can also spoon in the pastry to cover the sides of the dish and give a more peaky surface.

To make one large gougère, use a deep 20 cm (8 inch) round ovenproof dish and bake for 30–35 minutes.

Fish and chips

Tradition at its best: firm white fish that flakes at the touch of a fork, cooked in a crisp batter and served with home-made chips. For the best results, make sure that the fish is really fresh and eat piping hot.

*Preparation time **20 minutes** + **30 minutes standing***
*Total cooking time **20 minutes***
Serves 4

600 g (1¼ lb) floury potatoes, peeled
oil, for deep-frying
4 x 150–180 g (5–5¾ oz) pieces firm white
  fish fillet, skinned
2–3 tablespoons seasoned flour
lemon wedges, to garnish

BATTER
160 g (5¼ oz) cornflour
160 g (5¼ oz) plain flour
3 teaspoons baking powder
315–500 ml (10–16 fl oz) beer

1   Cut the potatoes into 5–10 mm (¼–½ inch) wide, 1 cm (½ inch) deep and 6–8 cm (2½–3 inch) long batons. Place in a bowl and cover with cold water.

2   To make the batter, sift the cornflour, plain flour, baking powder and some salt and black pepper into a bowl and make a well in the centre. Gradually pour in the beer, using a wooden spoon to beat it into the flour, until the mixture becomes a smooth batter the consistency of cream (the amount of liquid you need will depend on the flour you use). Cover and leave for 30 minutes at room temperature.

3   Meanwhile, fill a deep-fat fryer or heavy-based pan one third full of oil and heat to 160–170°C (315–325°F) (a cube of bread dropped into the oil will brown in 30 seconds). Drain and pat the chips dry, then fry until the bubbles subside and the chips have formed a thin, light-golden skin. Lift out the chips, allowing excess oil to drip back into the fryer, and transfer the chips onto crumpled paper towels.

4   Increase the temperature of the oil to 180°C (350°F) (a cube of bread dropped into the oil will brown in 15 seconds). Wash the fish and dry thoroughly on paper towels. Place the seasoned flour on a plate and coat the fish, shaking off the excess. Dip the fish into the batter until it is evenly coated, then lift out using fingers or forks to allow any excess mixture to drip off. Lower the fish carefully into the fryer or pan and fry, in batches if necessary, for 5 minutes, or until golden and crisp. Do not overcrowd the pan or the temperature will be lowered. Remove and drain on crumpled paper towels. Season with salt, place on a wire rack and keep warm.

5   Place the chips in the oil again and fry until golden and crisp. Remove and drain, season with salt and serve with the fish, lemon wedges and tartare or tomato sauce.

Sole Véronique with potato galettes

A classic French recipe using white grapes in a white wine sauce to accompany poached lemon sole. Here the dish is served on crisp potato galettes.

Preparation time **1 hour**
Total cooking time **1 hour 15 minutes**
Serves 4

POTATO GALETTES
**500 g (1 lb) floury potatoes, peeled and cut
  into even-sized pieces**
4 egg whites
clarified butter or ghee, for frying

8 x 85 g (2³/4 oz) lemon sole fillets
2 French shallots, finely chopped
100 ml (3¹/4 fl oz) dry white wine
200 ml (6¹/2 fl oz) fish stock
200 g (6¹/2 oz) seedless white grapes
300 ml (10 fl oz) cream

1 To make the potato galettes, place the potatoes in a large pan of salted, cold water. Cover and bring to the boil, then reduce the heat and simmer for about 15–20 minutes, or until the potatoes are tender to the point of a sharp knife. Drain, return to the pan and shake over low heat for 1–2 minutes to remove excess moisture. Mash or push through a fine sieve, season with salt and black pepper and cool.

2 Meanwhile, wash the sole and dry well on paper towels. Fold the skinned side under at each end of the fillets to give eight fillets about 10 cm (4 inches) long. Butter a shallow 30 x 21 cm (12 x 8¹/2 inch) ovenproof dish and sprinkle half the shallots over the base. Place the sole on the shallots, drizzle with one tablespoon each of the wine and stock and season lightly with some salt and black pepper. Cover with plastic wrap and set aside in the refrigerator.

3 Put the grapes in a pan of boiling water and cook for 15 seconds, then drain and plunge into iced water to cool. Remove from the water, peel away their skins and reserve the grapes and skins separately.

4 Preheat the oven to moderate 180°C (350°F/Gas 4). In a bowl, whisk the egg whites until they hold in stiff peaks. Stir a quarter of the egg white into the potato then, using a spatula or large metal spoon, gently fold in the remaining egg white.

5 Place a 1 cm (¹/2 inch) depth of clarified butter or ghee in a large heavy-based frying pan and place over moderate heat. Lightly oil the inside of an 8 cm (3 inch) round plain pastry cutter and place it in the pan. Place a 5 mm (¹/4 inch) layer of the potato inside the cutter. Gently loosen around the sides with a palette knife and lift the cutter away. Repeat to fill the pan, leaving enough space between the galettes to turn them. Fry for 5 minutes each side, or until golden brown. Drain on crumpled paper towels, then remove to a wire rack in a low oven and keep warm.

6 Place the remaining shallots, wine and stock in a pan. Add the grape skins, bring to the boil, then simmer for 20 minutes, or until the mixture is syrupy. Meanwhile, bake the sole for 10–12 minutes, or until opaque and cooked through. Stir the cream into the sauce and simmer for 5 minutes, or until syrupy, then strain into a clean pan, discarding the grape skins. Strain the cooking liquid from the fish into the sauce, reduce again to syrupy, then add the grapes and warm through.

7 To serve, place a galette on each plate, arrange two sole fillets on top and coat with the sauce.

Chef's tip For a richer finish, mix together 3 tablespoons lightly whipped cream and 1 egg yolk. Coat the sauced fillets with the mixture, then grill to golden brown.

Smoked salmon and leek terrine with sauce verte

Beautifully light but with a good depth of flavour, this dish makes a perfect appetizer or lunch. Cooking the leeks in fish stock helps them to press together and makes it easier to slice the terrine.

Preparation time **1 hour + 4 hours refrigeration**
Total cooking time **20 minutes**
Serves 10

1.5 litres fish stock
30 very small whole leeks, trimmed of tough
   green leaves and roots
10–15 large spinach leaves, stalks removed
560 g (1 lb 2 oz) long slices of smoked salmon
rocket leaves, to garnish

SAUCE VERTE
105 g (3¹/2 oz) watercress, tough stems removed
45 g (1¹/2 oz) fresh chervil leaves, chopped
45 g (1¹/2 oz) fresh dill leaves, chopped
45 g (1¹/2 oz) fresh parsley
few drops of lemon juice
350 ml (11 fl oz) crème fraîche or sour cream

1 In a large pan, bring the fish stock to the boil. Place the leeks in stock, reduce the temperature and gently simmer for 20 minutes, or until tender. Drain well, then set aside to cool.

2 Blanch the spinach in boiling water for 30 seconds. Drain, then plunge into iced water. Carefully lift the leaves out individually and place on paper towels or a cloth and pat dry.

3 Line a 1-litre, 21 x 10 cm (8¹/2 x 4 inch) terrine mould with plastic wrap, then line the base and sides with some of the smoked salmon, allowing a long overhang at one end. Add a layer of spinach, allowing for an overlap over one side of the terrine.

4 Tightly pack two layers of leeks lengthways into the bottom of the lined terrine and season well, then add a layer of half the remaining salmon, followed by one layer of leeks and seasoning. Cover with the remaining salmon and top this with two layers of leeks and seasoning. Fold over the salmon and spinach overhangs to enclose the filling and cover with plastic wrap. Cut a piece of cardboard to fit inside the terrine, cover it twice with foil and place a 1 kg (2 lb) weight on top (this can be cans). Refrigerate for 4 hours.

5 To prepare the sauce verte, place the watercress, herbs and a little water into a blender and blend to a fine purée. Push through a coarse sieve, add the lemon juice and salt and black pepper and fold in the crème fraîche. Cover with plastic wrap and place in the refrigerator until ready to serve.

6 To serve, slice the terrine and arrange on plates with a spoonful of the sauce verte and some rocket leaves to garnish.

Fish minestrone with pesto

A twist on the classic Italian soup, with the addition of scallops, prawns and a dash of cream. The pesto is stirred through at the end and any extra can be tossed through pasta for a great midweek dinner.

Preparation time **1 hour 15 minutes**
Total cooking time **15 minutes**
Serves 4

4 fresh scallops
12 tiger prawns, shells on
1 litre fish stock
2¹/2 tablespoons olive oil
1 small onion, finely diced
1 small carrot, diced
¹/2 swede, diced
1 small turnip, diced
1 potato, diced
¹/4 celeriac, diced
50 g (1³/4 oz) small pasta shapes,
   such as ditalini
25 g (³/4 oz) French beans, cut into
   5 mm (¹/4 inch) lengths
1 zucchini (courgette), diced
3 tablespoons cream
50 g (1³/4 oz) cooked or canned flageolet beans
few sprigs of fresh chervil, to garnish

PESTO
55 g (1³/4 oz) garlic
55 g (1³/4 oz) pine kernels, toasted
35 g (1¹/4 oz) grated Parmesan
30 g (1 oz) fresh basil leaves
45 g (1¹/2 oz) fresh parsley leaves
200 ml (6¹/2 fl oz) olive oil

1 To prepare the scallops, follow the method in the Chef's techniques on page 62. Place the scallops flat on a board and slice each one into three circles, leaving the orange roe whole. Shell and devein the prawns, following the method in the Chef's techniques on page 60. Cover and refrigerate until needed.

2 To make the pesto, put all the ingredients in a blender or food processor and blend to a smooth thick mixture. Transfer to a clean screw-top jar and cover the surface with a layer of oil to stop it oxidizing.

3 Place the stock in a small pan and bring to the boil. Heat the oil in a large pan, add the onion, carrot and swede, cover and cook over low heat for 2 minutes, or until soft and translucent. Add the turnip and potato, pour in the boiling stock, season lightly with salt and bring to the boil. Add the celeriac and pasta and simmer for 5 minutes, or until the vegetables are just tender. Add the beans and zucchini and cook for 2 minutes.

4 Remove from the heat and stir in the cream and flageolet beans. Add 3 tablespoons of the pesto, the scallops and prawns and mix gently to blend in the pesto. Season with salt and black pepper, then return to the stove just to bring back to the boil (do not continue to cook or the scallops and prawns will overcook and toughen). Garnish with chervil sprigs to serve.

Chef's tip Leftover pesto will keep in the refrigerator for up to one week or it can be stored in the freezer in an airtight container. Toss with pasta, use as a salad dressing or place on cooked mussels in the half shell and quickly grill until bubbling.

Creamy and salsa oysters

Two versions of classic oyster dishes. The creamy version is made with cream, white wine and bacon and is flashed under the grill to give a golden topping. If you prefer less heat, just omit the chilli. The salsa oysters are not cooked and come with a fiery tomato, red onion and lime dressing.

Preparation time **50 minutes**
Total cooking time **15 minutes (Creamy)**
Serves 4

24 oysters

CREAMY
2 teaspoons Tabasco
120 g (4 oz) bacon rashers, rind removed
4 egg yolks
100 ml (3¹/4 fl oz) white wine
80 ml (2³/4 fl oz) thick (double) cream,
  lightly whipped
¹/2 red chilli, seeded and finely chopped
1 tablespoon olive oil
1 small red capsicum (pepper), cut into matchsticks

OR

SALSA
410 g (13 oz) ripe tomatoes, peeled, seeded
  and diced
1 red onion, finely chopped
juice of 2 limes
1 teaspoon Tabasco
1 teaspoon roughly chopped fresh coriander
3 teaspoons roughly chopped fresh flat-leaf parsley
fresh coriander leaves, to garnish

1 Shuck the oysters following the method in the Chef's techniques on page 60. Add the oysters to their liquid in the bowl and refrigerate. Clean the deeper half of the shells thoroughly and discard the flat halves.

2 To make the creamy oysters, add half the Tabasco to the oysters before refrigerating. Place the bacon in a small pan, cover with cold water, bring to the boil and simmer for 4 minutes. Drain, then run under cold water to remove excess salt. Tip the bacon onto paper towels to drain, then cut into matchsticks.

3 Place the egg yolks, wine and remaining Tabasco in a heatproof bowl over a pan of simmering water, ensuring the bowl is not touching the water. Whisk vigorously until the mixture has increased to three or four times the original volume and leaves a trail across the surface when lifted on the whisk. Remove the bowl from the pan, whisk until it cools to room temperature, then fold in the cream and chilli and set aside.

4 Preheat the grill. Heat the oil in a pan and fry the bacon until golden, then add the capsicum and cook over medium heat for 1 minute, or until soft but not coloured. Heat the oysters and their juices in another pan over low heat for 1 minute. Do not overheat or the oysters will toughen. Put the warm oysters back in their shells and place in an ovenproof dish (a layer of rock salt underneath will help them stay balanced). Pour over the juices and place the bacon and capsicum mixture on top. Spoon the egg mixture over and place under the grill for 2 minutes, or until golden. Serve immediately.

5 To make the salsa, mix together all the ingredients except the whole coriander leaves with some salt and black pepper. Cover with plastic wrap and set aside for 20 minutes at room temperature. Place an oyster in each shell and spoon over some juices and a little salsa, then garnish with a coriander leaf. Arrange on a bed of salad leaves or crushed ice.

Creamy oysters (top) and Salsa oysters

Spaghetti marinara

Meaning 'Mariner's style', the name of this pasta dish originated from fishermen's wives throwing their husbands' daily catch into a quick tomato, garlic, herb and olive oil sauce.

*Preparation time **35 minutes***
*Total cooking time **50 minutes***
Serves 4

3 tablespoons olive oil
I onion, finely chopped
2 cloves garlic, crushed
I tablespoon tomato paste
2 x 400 g (12³/4 oz) cans chopped tomatoes
2 sprigs of fresh thyme
I bay leaf
**250 g (8 oz) fresh tuna, skinned and cut
    into 2 cm (³/4 inch) cubes**
**250 g (8 oz) squid tubes, sliced into 5 mm
    (¹/4 inch) rings**
**250 g (8 oz) white crab meat, drained
    well if frozen**
4 tablespoons chopped fresh basil leaves
500 g (I lb) spaghetti

1   In a large pan, heat 2 tablespoons of the olive oil, add the onion and garlic and cook for 4 minutes, or until the onion is soft and translucent. Stir in the tomato paste and cook for a further minute. Add the tomatoes, thyme and bay leaf, season with salt and black pepper, then bring to the boil, lower the heat and simmer for about 25 minutes.

2   Heat the remaining oil in a large frying pan, add the tuna and toss over high heat for about 3 minutes, or until lightly cooked. Lift out the tuna using a slotted spoon and drain in a colander over a bowl. Reheat the oil remaining in the pan, add the squid rings and toss over high heat for 3 minutes, or until opaque, then remove and add to the tuna to drain.

3   Remove and discard the thyme and bay leaf from the tomato sauce, then add the tuna, squid, crab meat and 3 tablespoons of the basil. Stir gently to combine without breaking up the fish and season with salt and black pepper. Remove from the heat and keep warm.

4   Meanwhile, bring a large pan of salted water to the boil. Add a splash of oil to stop the pasta sticking and cook the spaghetti according to the manufacturer's instructions. Drain well.

5   Serve the spaghetti on warm plates and spoon the marinara sauce on top. Sprinkle with the remaining basil and serve immediately.

Chef's tip Frying the seafood at a high temperature will seal it, give a good flavour and allow it to hold its shape.

'Lasagne' of salmon with tomato and spinach

There is no pasta in this special dish, but the effect is like a lasagne, with layers of pink salmon, dark-green spinach leaves, white and tomato sauces making for a stunning dinner-party recipe.

*Preparation time **1 hour***
*Total cooking time **1 hour 15 minutes***
*Serves **4***

4 x 150 g (5 oz) thick centre cuts of fresh salmon fillet,
skinned and cut into 3 slices horizontally
(ask your fishmonger to do this)
90 ml (3 fl oz) olive oil
2 onions, finely chopped
1 kg (2 lb) ripe tomatoes, peeled, seeded and diced
2 cloves garlic, crushed
bouquet garni (see Chef's tip)
45 g (1¹/2 oz) unsalted butter
750 g (1¹/2 lb) fresh spinach
a small pinch of nutmeg
12 small black olives, halved and pitted, to garnish
few sprigs of fresh chervil, to garnish

BEURRE BLANC
3 French shallots, finely chopped
315 ml (10 fl oz) white wine
3 tablespoons cider vinegar
1 tablespoon thick (double) cream or crème fraîche
180 g (5³/4 oz) unsalted butter, cut into small
cubes and chilled
2 tablespoons finely chopped fresh chives

WHITE SAUCE
15 g (¹/2 oz) unsalted butter
15 g (¹/2 oz) plain flour
250 ml (8 fl oz) milk

1 Separate the slices of salmon, brush with olive oil, cover and place in the refrigerator. Heat the oil in a pan, add the onion, cover and cook for 4 minutes, or until soft and translucent. Stir in the tomato, garlic, bouquet garni and some salt and black pepper. Cook for about 40 minutes, stirring occasionally, until the mixture is thick. Discard the bouquet garni, re-season and keep warm.

2 To make the beurre blanc, place the shallots, wine and vinegar in a pan, bring to the boil and cook to reduce by a quarter. Add the cream and remove from the heat, then whisk in the butter a piece at a time until you have a creamy, flowing sauce that coats the back of a spoon. Strain into a bowl, stir in the chives, cover with plastic wrap and sit over a pan of warm water.

3 To make the white sauce, melt the butter in a heavy-based pan over low-medium heat. Sprinkle the flour over the butter and cook for 1–2 minutes without allowing it to colour, stirring continuously with a wooden spoon. Remove the pan from the heat and slowly add the milk, whisking to avoid lumps. Return to medium heat and bring to the boil, stirring constantly. Cook for 3–4 minutes, or until the sauce coats the back of a spoon. Cover and keep warm. Preheat the grill.

4 Melt the butter in a large frying pan or wok, add the spinach and toss over high heat for 2 minutes, or until wilted. Add the nutmeg, salt and black pepper and place in a sieve over a bowl to allow the moisture to drain through. Season the fish and grill for 1 minute each side.

5 To serve, take four plates and place a salmon slice on each one. Using half the spinach, spread a layer on each slice, then add half the white sauce, followed by half the tomato sauce. Cover with another slice of fish, the remaining spinach, white and tomato sauce, and finish with the remaining salmon. Spoon the beurre blanc around the base of the plate and garnish with the olive halves and chervil leaves.

Chef's tip To make a bouquet garni, wrap the green part of a leek loosely around a bay leaf, a sprig of thyme, some celery leaves and a few stalks of parsley, then tie with string, leaving a long tail for easy removal.

Snapper with fennel en papillote

Cooked in a parcel of greaseproof paper or foil to retain all the juices and flavours, the white wine, basil leaves and gentle anise flavour of fennel infuse the sweet snapper or mullet.

Preparation time **40 minutes**
Total cooking time **35 minutes**
Serves 4

**2 x 400 g (12³/4 oz) snapper or red mullet,
filleted (see page 63)**
2 large fennel bulbs
60 g (2 oz) unsalted butter
16 fresh basil leaves
80 ml (2³/4 fl oz) white wine
4 teaspoons Pastis or Ricard (optional)

1 Wash the fish, dry on paper towels and refrigerate until needed. With a small sharp knife, trim off the small stalks at the top of the fennel bulbs, keeping the leaves and discarding the thick stalks. With a large sharp knife, cut the bulb in half from the top down through the root, then cut away and discard the root. Cut the fennel into 5 mm (¹/4 inch) thick slices.

2 Heat the butter in a pan, add the fennel, cover and cook over low heat for 25 minutes, or until soft to the point of a sharp knife. Remove from the stove and season with salt and black pepper. Preheat the oven to hot 220°C (425°F/Gas 7).

3 Fold a piece of greaseproof paper or foil in two, then cut out a large half tear-drop shape, 5 cm (2 inches) bigger than the fish. Open the paper or foil out and you should have a heart shape. Repeat to make four in total, then lay the shapes flat and brush with melted butter. Spoon the fennel onto one side of each heart and spread to the size of the fish. Place a fish fillet on top and lightly season with salt and black pepper. Arrange four basil leaves on each piece of fish, then sprinkle each one with a tablespoon of white wine and a teaspoon of Pastis or Ricard. Top with the reserved sprigs of fennel leaf.

4 Immediately fold the empty side of paper or foil over the fish and seal the edges by twisting and folding tightly. Place on a baking tray or in a shallow ovenproof dish and bake for 5–8 minutes.

5 Place the parcels on plates and allow your guests to open them and release the aromas.

Chef's tip Other fish can be cooked by this method, such as perch, mackerel or cod. The cooking times will vary according to the thickness and shape of the fish.

Thai green fish curry

This fish curry is prepared with an easy-to-make home-made green curry paste, which gives a fresh, authentic Thai taste. Serve with steamed jasmine fragrant rice.

Preparation time **15 minutes**
Total cooking time **20 minutes**
Serves 4–6

GREEN CURRY PASTE
250 g (8 oz) coconut milk
8 small green chillies (bird's-eye), halved and seeded
I stalk lemon grass, chopped
2 tablespoons lime juice
25 g (³/4 oz) galangal or ginger, sliced
I teaspoon ground coriander
¹/2 teaspoon ground cumin
5 Asian shallots or spring onions, peeled and chopped
3 kaffir lime leaves, chopped

I tablespoon sunflower oil
¹/2 mild red or green chilli, seeded and
   cut into shreds
25 g (³/4 oz) drained green peppercorns in brine,
   plus I teaspoon of brine
I teaspoon sugar
400 ml (12³/4 fl oz) can coconut milk
5 kaffir lime leaves
750 g (1¹/2 lb) firm white fish fillets, skinned
   and cut into 4 cm (1¹/2 inch) cubes

I tablespoon fish sauce
2 tablespoons roughly torn basil leaves, for garnish

1 To make the green curry paste, blend all the ingredients in a blender or food processor, scraping down the sides of the bowl occasionally, until the mixture is smooth and forms a thick paste. If it is too thick, add a little more coconut milk or a few drops of sunflower oil. Place in a bowl, cover and set aside.
2 In a wok or large frying pan, heat the sunflower oil, then add the chilli and toss for about 4 minutes, or until lightly golden. Add the peppercorns, brine, sugar and coconut milk, bring to the boil and simmer for about 3 minutes.
3 Add 4 tablespoons of the green curry paste, the lime leaves and the fish. Simmer for 5–10 minutes, or until the fish is cooked. Remove and discard the lime leaves, season with salt, black pepper and the fish sauce and keep warm.
4 To serve, lift out the fish into a warm serving dish and spoon the sauce over. Sprinkle with the basil and serve with steamed jasmine rice.

Chef's tip The leftover curry paste can be stored in an airtight container in the freezer and used to make a fish, chicken or vegetable green curry.

Seafood pie

A classic family dish, this seafood pie is made with white fish, mussels and prawns in a light wine sauce, topped with a purée of potato that is baked to lightly golden in the oven.

Preparation time **50 minutes**
Total cooking time **1 hour 10 minutes**
Serves 6

500 g (1 lb) mussels, scrubbed and beards removed
** (see page 62)**
150 g (5 oz) raw prawns, shells on
60 g (2 oz) unsalted butter
2 French shallots, finely chopped
1 leek, white part only, cut into julienne strips
** (see Chef's tips)**
220 ml (7 fl oz) dry white wine
500 ml (16 fl oz) milk
1 onion, studded with 1 clove
bouquet garni (see Chef's tips)
600 g (1 1/4 lb) mixed firm white fish fillets, such
** as lemon sole, plaice, cod and halibut, skinned**
** and cut into 3 cm (1 1/4 inch) cubes**
30 g (1 oz) plain flour
1 kg (2 lb) floury potatoes, peeled and cut into pieces
50 g (1 3/4 oz) unsalted butter, extra
1 egg yolk
4 tablespoons cream
small pinch of ground nutmeg

1 Place the mussels in a cool place covered with a damp cloth. Shell and devein the prawns, following the method in the Chef's techniques on page 60.

2 In a pan, melt half the butter over low heat, then add the shallots, cover and cook for 2–3 minutes, or until soft. Add the leek and cook for 2 minutes, uncovered, then add a tablespoon of the wine and simmer until the liquid has evaporated. Place the mixture in a shallow oval 28 x 20 cm (11 x 8 inch) ovenproof dish.

3 Place the mussels and remaining wine in a pan, bring slowly to the boil, covered, and cook for 2–3 minutes, or until all the mussels are open. Discard any unopened mussels. Drain, reserving the cooking liquid, then remove the mussels from their shells and scatter into the dish. Strain the liquid through a sieve lined with muslin or a damp piece of paper towel and set aside.

4 Add the milk, onion and bouquet garni to a pan, bring to barely simmering and cook for 5 minutes. Remove the onion and bouquet garni and add the fish, prawns and reserved mussel liquid. Heat to just simmering and poach the seafood for 2 minutes. Drain, reserving the liquid and keeping it hot, and add the seafood to the dish.

5 Melt the remaining butter in a pan over low heat, sprinkle over the flour and cook, stirring, for 1 minute without colouring. Remove from the heat and blend in the hot poaching liquid. Return to medium heat, bring to the boil, stirring constantly, and cook for 3–4 minutes, or until it thickens and coats the back of a spoon. Season, then pour over the fish. Cover and refrigerate.

6 Preheat the oven to moderate 180°C (350°F/Gas 4). Place the potatoes in a pan of salted, cold water, cover and bring to the boil, then reduce the heat and simmer for 15–20 minutes, or until the potatoes are tender to a sharp knife. Drain, return to the pan and shake over low heat for 1–2 minutes to remove excess moisture. Mash or push through a fine sieve back into the pan, then beat in the extra butter, yolk and finally the cream. Season with nutmeg, salt and black pepper, spoon into a piping bag with a large star nozzle and pipe a pattern over the surface of the fish, or spread the potato, then use a fork to peak it. Bake for 30 minutes, or until lightly golden.

Chef's tips Julienne strips are strips of vegetables, the size and shape of matchsticks.

To make a bouquet garni, wrap the green part of a leek loosely around a bay leaf, a sprig of thyme, some celery leaves and a few stalks of parsley, then tie with string, leaving a long tail for easy removal.

Seafood gumbo

A thick, spicy soup from the American South with its origins in Creole cuisine, influenced by African and French cooking. The original meaning of 'Gumbo' was okra, and this vegetable is what thickens the dish.

*Preparation time **45 minutes***
*Total cooking time **35 minutes***
Serves 4

12 tiger prawns, shells on
50 g (1³/4 oz) long-grain rice
2¹/2 tablespoons vegetable oil
2 large onions, chopped
1 celery stick, finely chopped
2 cloves garlic, crushed
1 red capsicum (pepper), diced
1 green capsicum (pepper), diced
3 tablespoons tomato paste
1 litre fish stock
2 teaspoons chopped fresh oregano
1 cooked crab in its shell, cleaned and cut
   into quarters or 4 cooked crab claws
   in their shells (see Chef's tip)
250 g (8 oz) okra, cut into 1 cm (¹/2 inch)
   round slices
150 g (5 oz) snapper or red mullet fillet, skinned
   and cut into 4 cm (1¹/2 inch) pieces
1 teaspoon Tabasco
1 teaspoon Worcestershire sauce
2 spring onions, finely chopped

1 Shell and devein the tiger prawns, leaving the tails intact, following the method in the Chef's techniques on page 60. Cook the rice in boiling salted water for 10 minutes, or until tender, drain and leave to cool.

2 In a large frying pan, heat the oil. Add the onion, celery, garlic and capsicum. Stir over medium heat for 5 minutes, or until soft but not coloured. Mix in the tomato paste and stir for 1 minute, then add the stock, oregano and crab and simmer for 5 minutes. Gently stir in the okra, season lightly, cover and simmer for 15–20 minutes, or until the okra is tender.

3 Remove the pan from the stove and lift out the crab pieces, crack them with the base of a small heavy pan, and remove the meat as whole pieces if possible. Discard the shells, cover the crab meat and keep warm.

4 Skim the gumbo to remove any oil or foam, then return to the stove, add the fish and prawns and simmer for 2 minutes. Add the Tabasco and Worcestershire sauces, stir in the rice and bring the gumbo back to simmering. Taste and add more salt, pepper or sauces if necessary (the soup should have a good hint of chilli). To serve, ladle into bowls and garnish with spring onion. Serve with bread.

Chef' tip To clean a crab, remove the stomach sac and grey spongy fingers (gills).

Lobster américaine

One of the most famous of all lobster dishes, where the lobster is cooked on the shell in a rich tomato and wine sauce. There is much dispute on the origins of the name—whether it should be 'Armoricaine', the ancient name for Brittany in France, or 'Américaine', after a French chef who had worked in America.

Preparation time **30 minutes**
Total cooking time **50 minutes**
Serves 4

4 x 500 g (1 lb) lobsters or 2 x 800 g–1 kg
  (1 lb 10 oz–2 lb) lobsters
100 ml (3¼ fl oz) vegetable oil
45 g (1½ oz) unsalted butter
1 onion, diced
1 carrot, diced
2 celery sticks, diced
150 ml (5 fl oz) dry white wine
2½ tablespoons brandy
500 ml (16 fl oz) fish stock
3 tablespoons tomato paste
500 g (1 lb) ripe tomatoes, halved and seeded
1 bouquet garni (see Chef's tips)
fresh parsley, to garnish

1 If you have bought live lobsters, kill them according to the method in the Chef's techniques on page 61. If you prefer not to do this, ask your fishmonger to do it.
2 Prepare the lobster following the method in the Chef's techniques on page 61. To fry the lobster claws and tails, heat the oil in a large frying pan and add the claws and tails. Fry quickly, turning with long-handled tongs, until they change colour from blue to red and the tail flesh shrinks visibly from the shell. Lift them out of the pan onto a plate and continue to prepare the lobster according to the method on page 61.
3 Heat half the butter in the pan and fry the pieces of head shell quickly until the colour has changed, as before. Remove any flesh and set aside. Add the reserved shell from the tail with the onion, carrot and celery and cook for about 5 minutes, or until lightly brown. Add the wine and reduce by half before adding the brandy and stock. Stir in the tomato paste and cook for 1 minute before adding the tomato halves. Cover the pan with a lid and, over gentle heat, cook for 20 minutes, or until the tomatoes are pulpy. While this is cooking, place the reserved coral and tomalley into a blender with the remaining butter and blend until smooth.
4 Remove the lid from the pan, add the bouquet garni and the reserved fried claws and cook for 10 minutes. Lift out the claws and cool before cracking to remove the flesh.
5 Strain the tomato mixture through a sieve into a clean pan, discarding the shell, tomato skins, bouquet garni and diced vegetables. Cook the tomato mixture, stirring occasionally, for 4 minutes, or until lightly syrupy.
6 Whisk the coral and tomalley flavoured butter into the sauce until smooth, then add the lobster tail flesh and simmer very gently for 1 minute (if overcooked, the flesh with be tough). Remove the pan from the stove and leave the lobster tail to rest for 5 minutes in the sauce before removing and slicing into round slices. Gently rewarm the slices in the sauce with all the cracked claw and head meat. To serve, spoon onto hot plates and garnish with the parsley.

Chef's tips To make a bouquet garni, wrap the green part of a leek loosely around a bay leaf, a sprig of thyme, some celery leaves and a few stalks of parsley, then tie with string, leaving a long tail for easy removal.

Lobsters generally have two large front claws. Although in some countries crayfish are also called lobsters, they do not have the large front claws.

Sole meunière

A stylish classic: the sole is quickly pan-fried, then butter and lemon juice is poured over and the fish is eaten hot with parsley and lemon wedges. Dover sole is recommended for its firm texture and succulence, but any flat fish could be substituted.

*Total preparation time **10 minutes***
*Total cooking time **10 minutes***
Serves 4

4 sole fillets, about 180–200 g
   (5³/4–6¹/2 oz) each, skinned
100 g (3¹/4 oz) clarified butter or ghee
100 g (3¹/4 oz) seasoned flour
100 g (3¹/4 oz) unsalted butter, chilled and
   cut into cubes
1 tablespoon lemon juice, strained
2 teaspoons finely chopped fresh parsley,
   to garnish
1 lemon, cut into wedges, to garnish

1 Wash the fish, then dry well on paper towels. In a large frying pan, heat the clarified butter until hot.

2 Place the seasoned flour on a plate and roll the fillets in it to coat thoroughly, then pat off any excess. Place in the pan, skinned-side-up, and fry for about 2 minutes, turning once, or until lightly golden. Remove and place on hot plates.

3 Drain off the hot butter used for frying and wipe out the pan with paper towels before returning to the heat. Add the butter to the pan and cook until golden and frothy. Remove from the stove, immediately add the lemon juice and, while still bubbling, spoon or pour over the fish.

4 Garnish with some parsley and serve immediately with the lemon wedges.

Basque-style tuna

Typically this Basque dish contains capsicums, onions, tomatoes and ham—ideal ingredients to match the meaty texture of fresh tuna.

Total preparation time **1 hour 5 minutes**
Total cooking time **20 minutes**
Serves 4

250 g (8 oz) ripe tomatoes
3 tablespoons olive oil
15 g (¹/2 oz) unsalted butter
4 x 185 g (6 oz) pieces tuna, skinned
2 onions, thinly sliced
1 small red capsicum (pepper), thinly sliced
1 small yellow capsicum (pepper), thinly sliced
1 small green capsicum (pepper), thinly sliced
3 cloves garlic, finely chopped
155 ml (5 fl oz) dry white wine
1 bouquet garni (see Chef's tip)
155 g (5 oz) Bayonne or Parma ham, thinly sliced and cut
    into 3 cm (1¹/4 inch) pieces
¹/2 tablespoon chopped fresh parsley, to garnish

1 Bring a small pan of water to the boil. With the point of a sharp knife, score a small cross on the skin at the base of each tomato. Drop into the boiling water for 10 seconds, then plunge into a bowl of iced water. Peel the skin away from the cross, then cut around and remove the stalk. Cut the tomatoes into quarters and discard the seeds. Roughly chop the tomato flesh.

2 In a large frying pan, heat 2 tablespoons of the oil and the butter. When foaming, add the tuna and fry over high heat for 1 minute each side, or until lightly golden. Remove from the pan. Add the onion, cover and cook over low heat, stirring occasionally, for 3–4 minutes, or until soft but not coloured. Add the capsicum and garlic and cook gently for 1 minute, or until soft. Return the fish to the pan, add the tomato, wine, bouquet garni and some salt. Cover and simmer for 5 minutes.

3 Remove the tuna and cover with foil to keep warm. Bring the mixture in the pan to the boil and cook rapidly to reduce for about 5 minutes, or until the liquid lightly coats the back of a spoon. Season with black pepper and a little more salt if necessary. Heat the remaining oil in a frying pan, add the ham and quickly fry for about 10 seconds each side (you may need to do this in batches, adding a little extra oil if necessary).

4 To serve, place the fish on plates and spoon the vegetable mixture over. Scatter the ham over or around the fish and sprinkle with the parsley.

Chef's tip To make a bouquet garni, wrap the green part of a leek loosely around a bay leaf, a sprig of thyme, some celery leaves and a few stalks of parsley, then tie with string, leaving a long tail for easy removal.

Chef's techniques

◆

Shucking oysters

Use a shucker with a protection shield and always protect the hand holding the oyster with a thick cloth.

Scrub the oysters in cold water. Place an oyster, rounded-side-down, on a thick doubled cloth in the palm of your hand.

Insert an oyster knife through the pointed end of the oyster at the hinge where the top and bottom shells meet. Work the knife in until at least 3 cm (1 1/4 inches) is inside. Twist the knife to separate the shells.

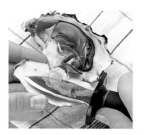

Slide the knife between the oyster and the top shell, cut through the hinge muscle and remove the top shell.

Slide the knife between the oyster and the bottom shell to release it. Remove the oyster and tip any liquid through a muslin-lined sieve into a bowl to get rid of any sand. Reserve the liquid.

Preparing prawns

If using raw prawns, remove the dark intestinal vein, which is unpleasant to eat.

Peel off the shell, being careful to keep the flesh intact. Leave the tail end intact if specified in the recipe.

Make a shallow cut along the back of the prawn with a small knife to expose the dark intestinal vein.

Remove the vein with the tip of a knife and discard. Rinse the prawns and pat dry with paper towels.

Preparing lobster bisque

The shell is an important part of the flavouring for this soup and is cooked with the meat.

Cut the lobsters in half lengthways. Remove and discard the sac in the head and the vein down the centre of the tail.

Twist off the claws and bat them with a rolling pin or the base of a small heavy pan to crack them.

Using a large sharp knife, cut across the tail into three or four pieces.

Killing a lobster

Place the lobster in the freezer for about 2 hours to desensitize it.

Hold the lobster tail down under a heavy cloth. Using a large sharp knife, place the point in the centre of the head and quickly pierce right through to the board, cutting down and forward between the eyes.

Preparing lobster américaine

Depending on the type of lobster you have, the claws will vary in size.

Twist and remove the two main claws, if applicable, from where they meet the body. Separate the head from the tail. Cook the claws and tail according to the method in the recipe.

Remove the flesh from the tail by snipping with scissors around the edge of the flat undershell and lifting it away.

Gently ease the flesh out of the tail in one piece using your fingers. Reserve the shell.

With a large sharp knife, split the head in two lengthways. Remove and reserve any coral (roe) and green-grey tomalley (liver). Discard the stomach sac found behind the mouth. Chop the head shell into large pieces.

Cleaning mussels

Mussels must be very carefully cleaned and should be stored in the refrigerator under a damp cloth.

Clean the mussels by scrubbing the shells with a brush to remove any sand. Scrape the barnacles off with a knife.

Pull off any beards from the mussels.

Discard any mussels that are broken, are not tightly closed or do not close when lightly tapped on a work surface.

Cleaning scallops

If the scallops are in their shells, remove them by sliding a knife under the white muscle and orange roe.

Wash the scallops to remove any grit or sand, then pull away the small tough shiny white muscle and the black vein, leaving the orange roe intact.

Filleting flat fish

Filleting your own fish is simple when you know how—just use a good sharp knife.

Lay the fish dark-side-up. Cut around the outside of the fish with a filleting knife where the flesh meets the fins.

Cut down the centre of the fish from head to tail with a sharp knife. Make sure you cut all the way through to the bone.

Working from the centre of the fillet to the edge, cut away one fillet with long broad strokes of the knife, without leaving too much flesh. Remove the other fillet in the same way, then turn the fish over and repeat.

Skinning fish

The angle of the knife against the skin is most important and skinning will then be easy.

Lay the fillet skin-side-down and cut across the flesh at the tail. Dip your fingers in salt to get a good grip, grasp the tail and, starting at the cut, work the knife away from you at a shallow angle using a sawing action.

Filleting round fish

Choose the freshest fish and fillet them yourself to be sure of the best-quality cut.

Cut off the fins and cut out the gills behind the head and discard.

Make a small cut at the bottom of the stomach, then cut along the underside, stopping just below the gills. Pull the innards out and discard. Rinse the inside of the fish out.

Make a cut around the back of the head, then working from head to tail, cut along the backbone. Holding the knife flat, use long strokes to cut away the flesh, then pull the flesh away from the bones.

Pin boning fish

Salmon or other fish, such as red mullet, often have small bones left in them. These need to be removed.

Run the fingers of your hand along the flesh, pressing lightly to find the bones. Remove any fine pin bones using a pair of tweezers or your fingers.

Serving a salmon

Place the cooked salmon on a piece of greaseproof paper before you begin.

Using a sharp knife, cut the skin just above the tail, then cut through the skin along the back and in front of the gills. Using the knife to help you, work from head to tail to peel off and discard the skin.

Place a serving plate under one side of the greaseproof paper and flip the fish over onto the plate, using the paper to help you. Remove the rest of the skin. Remove the head if preferred.

Scrape away any dark flesh with a knife. Split down the centre of the top fillet, then carefully remove and lay the two quarter fillets each side of the salmon.

Lift out the backbone by peeling it back from the head end. Snip it with scissors just before the tail. Remove any other stray bones and lift up and replace the two fillets.

Published by Bay Books, an imprint of Murdoch Books Pty Limited.

Murdoch Books and Le Cordon Bleu thank the 32 masterchefs of all the Le Cordon Bleu Schools, whose knowledge and expertise have made this book possible, especially: Chef Terrien, Chef Boucheret, Chef Duchêne (MOF), Chef Guillut, Chef Pinaud, Paris; Chef Males, Chef Walsh, Chef Power, Chef Neveu, Chef Paton, Chef Poole-Gleed, Chef Wavrin, London; Chef Chantefort, Chef Nicaud, Chef Jambert, Chef Honda, Tokyo; Chef Salambien, Chef Boutin, Chef Harris, Sydney; Chef Lawes, Adelaide; Chef Guiet, Chef Denis, Chef Petibon, Chef Jean Michel Poncet, Ottawa. Of the many students who helped the Chefs test each recipe, a special mention to graduates Hollace Hamilton and Alice Buckley. A very special acknowledgment to Helen Barnard, Alison Oakervee and Deepika Sukhwani, who have been responsible for the coordination of the Le Cordon Bleu team throughout this series under the Presidency of André Cointreau.

Murdoch Books Australia
Pier 8/9, 23 Hickson Rd,
Millers Point NSW 2000
Phone: +61 2 8220 2000
Fax: +61 2 8220 2558

Murdoch Books UK Limited
Erico House, 6th Floor North,
93-99 Upper Richmond Road
Putney, London SW15 2TG
Phone: +44 (0)20 8785 5995
Fax: +44 (0)20 8785 5985

ISBN-13: 978-1-921259-20-3
ISBN-10: 1-921259-20-5

Printed by SNP Leefung Printers Limited.
PRINTED IN CHINA.

This edition first published in 2006.

The Publisher and Le Cordon Bleu wish to thank Villeroy & Boch Australia Pty Ltd. and Waterford Wedgwood Australia Ltd. for their assistance in the photography
Front cover: Seafood paella

IMPORTANT INFORMATION

CONVERSION GUIDE

1 cup = 250 ml (8 fl oz)
1 Australian tablespoon = 20 ml (4 teaspoons)
1 UK tablespoon = 15 ml (3 teaspoons)

NOTE: We have used 20 ml tablespoons. If you are using a 15 ml tablespoon, for most recipes the difference will be negligible. For recipes using baking powder, gelatine, bicarbonate of soda and flour, add an extra teaspoon for each tablespoon specified.

CUP CONVERSIONS—DRY INGREDIENTS

1 cup flour, plain or self-raising = 125 g (4 oz)
1 cup sugar, caster = 250 g (8 oz)
1 cup breadcrumbs, dry = 125 g (4 oz)

IMPORTANT: Those who might be at risk from the effects of salmonella food poisoning (the elderly, pregnant women, young children and those suffering from immune deficiency diseases) should consult their GP with any concerns about eating raw eggs.